THE BRIDESMAID AND THE EX

Wedding Games: Book Two

KAYLA TIRRELL
DAPHNE JAMES HUFF

this is for Elle because she really is a superhero, and she can't edit this out because we added it after she proofread

ONE

5 Days Until Dream Wedding

HARPER SPEED WALKED through The Emerald Inn. Her entire body wanted to bolt down the hallway like a wedding cake was on fire, but she was afraid that kind of urgency so early in the morning would draw the attention of the production staff. And that was *not* what she needed right now.

It was supposed to be easy. Just take ten days off from work to film *Wedding Games* and get her sister Audrey the dream wedding she'd always wanted.

But now Audrey was missing. And Harper's Flour Girl Bakery was getting slammed with orders. Not to mention an even bigger surprise that Harper couldn't even let herself think about right now.

Harper had to focus. Bruce, the producer, couldn't find out the bride was MIA. He'd all but threatened to get the network's legal team involved if anything else went wrong. And this was a pretty big anything.

Harper had to make sure her sister was really gone before anyone else noticed.

First she looked for Audrey in her room. Miraculously, there were no cameramen around. Then she snuck out to the parking lot and discovered her older sister's car gone, and her luck held: no one from the production team was in the tech tent they'd set up outside. So, for now, it looked like her secret was safe.

But that didn't mean that things were okay. Not by a long shot.

Harper burst through the door of the dining hall, still secretly hoping Audrey would be sitting there with a cup of coffee and some fantastical excuse of why her car was missing. But instead, she found her youngest sister, Sienna, cozying up with Fox, the best man.

Harper would have much rather had privacy with Sienna, but she also knew Fox could be trusted. And thankfully, the only other people in the room were the maid of honor, Reagan, and her fiancé, Harry. And they were completely absorbed in a very heated discussion. Harper doubted they even registered her presence, even though she'd accidentally slammed the door against the wall when she came in.

Heck, even Sienna didn't seem to register Harper's presence, too absorbed in getting lost in Fox's light blue eyes. Barf. But what could Harper expect? Sienna and Fox had literally declared their feelings for each other the night before, and were in the gooey, disgusting honeymoon stage.

And they'd be the only ones on a honeymoon if Harper didn't fix this quick.

Harper tried to catch her breath. "Have either of you seen Audrey this morning?"

Sienna looked up and glared at Harper. "I've been kind of occupied. Isn't she in her room?"

Harper shook her head. "I've looked everywhere. And her car is missing."

Sienna stood up, all color draining from her face. And in that moment, Harper knew things were really bad. It wasn't just the stress of this week and everything that had come with filming *Wedding Games*.

Tears pooled in Harper's eyes. "I think...I think she's gone."

"Gone where?" Fox asked.

Harper shook her head frantically. "I don't know."

"How can you not know?" Sienna said, her eyes wide.

Harper tried not to take the question personally. Sienna was just as worried as she was. But it still stung because she *should* have known where Audrey was. The weight of Audrey's absence lay heavy on Harper's shoulders.

The three sisters were all three years apart, which was just enough so that they'd grown up in separate social worlds, rather than the best of friends that people liked to imagine when they saw the three of them together. But ever since Audrey had moved back to their hometown of Wellspring to teach, Harper and Audrey had made time to hang out and had discovered that, as adults, they had a ton in common. Their Sunday afternoons spent cupcake testing while lesson planning were the highlight of Harper's week.

At least, they had been the highlight until Eli finally popped the question, and Audrey became consumed with wedding planning. It had been fun at first. The two sisters talked flowers, bridesmaid dresses, and best of all, cake.

But when Audrey mentioned her engagement to a

parent at a school conference—who just happened to be one of the owners of The Emerald Inn—one thing led to another. And now the entire family was stuck on this stupid mountain filming a reality show. And all the sister time Harper and Audrey had been having went flying out the window.

It had been months since their last Sunday afternoon sister time. And now Audrey had run off in the middle of filming, and Harper didn't have a clue why or where.

It killed her that she didn't know what was going on with Audrey. But right now, she had to focus on doing what she did best and get everyone out of a sticky mess. Whether handling twenty last-minute orders at her bakery or keeping their weekly family dinners going, Harper could handle anything. Finding a missing bride should be a piece of cake.

So why did she just want to run up to her room and hide under the covers?

The door to the dining room burst open again, and Harper turned, hope fluttering in her stomach. But it wasn't Audrey running in crying about a flat tire. No, it was a tall, *handsome*, blond production assistant who looked perfectly refreshed.

Austin Mariani, the only guy she'd ever loved, looked just as delicious as he did every time Harper saw him—which was quite often these days considering he was a part of the *Wedding Games* crew. Hadn't *that* been a fun surprise the first day of filming?

"Is everything okay?" He looked from Sienna to Fox, then, after a beat too long, finally caught Harper's eye. She inhaled sharply, angry at herself for how his deep amber eyes still make her heart thump wildly after all these years.

No, everything most certainly was not okay. Her sister was missing, she didn't know where to find her, and now she was forced to stand right next to Austin, who, if his bland expression was any indication, had completely forgotten who she was. Her traitorous body leaned toward him, fondly remembering the days when he was hers.

He's not yours, he never was, you are over it.

She took a step back and straightened her shoulders. "Everything is fine," Harper said, her voice nearly cracking under the strain of appearing normal. She'd barely been coherent the past few days, on camera or off.

Sienna shot Harper a look before she put on a bright smile that Harper could barely tell was fake. She laced her hand through Fox's arm. "We were just waiting to hear what the plan is for today. The schedule just says 'dress day' so I assume the guys have a break today?"

"A break would be great," said Fox, his acting skills less convincing, but good nevertheless. "It's been hard to adjust to all these cameras around all the time."

Austin looked down at the clipboard in his hand. Harper hadn't seen him without it in the five days they'd been filming, but it didn't surprise her how attached to it he seemed to be. When she'd known him in college, he had been a super organized person. He'd always kept a calendar, and nothing ever slipped through the cracks. When projects were due, when exams were, the dates and locations of all the sorority parties across campus…

Back then, Harper had thought Austin knew everything. And it looked like some things never changed, because when he turned his gaze to Harper, the corners of his mouth turned down just the tiniest bit. He knew Sienna was lying.

She did her best to adopt the same carefree smile that Sienna still had plastered to her face, but his frown deepened. He looked down at the clipboard again briefly before looking back at Harper.

"Bruce should be down soon to go through today's schedule," he said.

At the mention of the producer's name, Harper felt a cool trickle of sweat make its way down her neck into her shirt. Did Bruce already know about Audrey? She casually wiped her hands on her jeans, but the clamminess didn't go away. She resisted the urge to do it again.

"Actually, Harper, I'm glad you're here," Austin continued. "Could you come with me, please? I have a quick question about some footage from the bakery the crew took the other day."

The footage from the bakery? The only thing they'd filmed inside Flour Girl was Harper rolling dough. There was nothing special or confusing about that. And even though Austin hadn't been there, he had seen her roll out dough hundreds of times in her college dorm. Maybe he just wanted to talk to her. A splash of hope surged through her, like a drop of red food coloring spreading through cake batter.

Then he lifted an eyebrow at her and jerked his head toward the door. A giant ball of dread settled in her stomach like a burned Christmas cookie. She'd forgotten he also knew what she looked like when she lied. Maybe she wasn't as forgettable as she'd thought. She certainly relived that painful graduation day over and over. Her embarrassing declaration of love. Maybe he did, too, and ignoring her the past few days was just his way of being nice.

Harper glanced over at Sienna and gave her what she hoped was a believable "everything will be totally fine" smile before she followed Austin out into the hall.

But deep down, she knew that it wouldn't.

TWO

5 Days Until Dream Wedding

AUSTIN STRUGGLED to keep his breathing steady and his hands from shaking as he led Harper down the hall. Ever since seeing her on the first day of filming, he'd been able to keep his distance from the one who got away—or rather the one he'd left behind like a total idiot.

But today, he'd finally gotten close enough to talk to her. And, after four years of silence, the first actual words out of his mouth were "is everything okay?"

Those three words weren't even close to the script he'd gone over in his head since realizing that the Harper Hudson on his contestant list was, in fact, the girl he'd been in love with four years ago. The same Harper Hudson he might *still* be in love with. Over the last few days he'd mentally prepared half a dozen speeches to apologize for the pain he caused her.

But when he'd finally come face to face with her, he'd chickened out and fallen back on what he knew— production. He treated her like any other seemingly spooked contestant and asked if she was okay.

Austin half expected Harper to reach out and slap his cheek, but she didn't. Her face flashed through several different emotions before settling on the face she always made when she was lying.

She *wasn't* okay.

Harper was keeping a secret, and that was a very dangerous thing to do on Bruce's set. The middle-aged producer was notorious for the way he demanded to be in control of every aspect of his shows. And this group of contestants wasn't doing a very good job of keeping Bruce happy.

They'd had one argumentative actress-wannabe question everything and go against his demands. Then all the groomsmen went on a late-night escapade that the whole crew was sure would give Bruce a coronary. But Bruce had worked his magic, and everything was good for now.

Unfortunately, none of the contestants knew the thin line they were currently toeing. Not in the same way Austin did. He'd heard the stories from Jennifer, one of the other production assistants, about what had happened to the reality show Bruce had been producing before *Wedding Games*—the one that never even made it to an editing studio.

So now, Austin needed to figure out what was going on with Harper before Bruce decided he'd had enough. Austin couldn't handle the idea of leaving another set and having to start all over again—especially now that he was so close to Harper again. And while he'd never met Audrey before filming began on *Wedding Games*, he didn't like the idea of Harper's sister having to deal with the consequences of a broken contract.

Harper trailed behind Austin down the hall toward

the safe room, her silence heavy and accusing. He was risking a lot by taking her there, but he knew she wasn't going to open up anywhere a camera could be lurking behind a corner. But he wasn't sure she would confess what was really going on in the small linen closet either.

Harper followed him inside without a word, but as soon as Austin shut and locked the door behind them, she crossed her arms and lifted a brow. "I thought we were looking at footage?"

"You knew that we weren't," he said with more bravado than he felt. He leaned back against the wall. It was a tiny space, and he was way too aware of how good Harper smelled. She hadn't been at the bakery in days, but it was like the delicious aroma of cinnamon and everything sweet just followed her around. "What didn't you tell me back there?"

Harper made the "get me out of this" face he knew so well. Or at least, had known so well. "There may be a problem with Audrey," she said, not quite meeting his eyes.

His chest squeezed. So, he'd been right to suspect something. He just hoped it wasn't anything serious. "You mean, like, she's sick?"

"Uh, not exactly." Harper looked down and shuffled her feet.

Austin bit his tongue. His first instinct was to ask a million questions and find out what was going on as quickly as possible, so that he could handle it in the same timely fashion. But he also knew Harper wasn't a person to be rushed. She took her time, which was great when she was decorating a cake or waiting for dough to rise, but it would be great if, just for once, she could be on his schedule.

"Audrey seems to be...missing."

Luckily, he was already leaning against the wall because Austin's legs threatened to give out. He had to get it together, for the sake of the show and everyone on it.

"Any idea where she's gone?" He winced a little at how stern he sounded. Why was it so hard to talk to her normally? He had no trouble giving directions to anyone else in the cast, but then again, he wasn't secretly in love with anyone else on the cast.

"If I did, I would be there getting her, wouldn't I?" Harper leveled her steely gray gaze on him and put her hands on her hips.

Austin swallowed hard. He'd forgotten how she could go from zero to pissed in about one point three seconds. He paused and tried to find a non-confrontational way to phrase his next question but didn't have much luck. "Do you know what you're going to do?"

"What am I going to do?" Harper shook her head and let out a harsh laugh. "Hmm, let's see. I need to go down to Flour Girl at some point today and make sure my staff filled the giant order for a birthday party, and that they're doing my prep for a wedding cake."

Austin nodded but didn't interrupt.

"Then I need to find a way to somehow lose the cameras to keep looking for my sister, even though they've mysteriously managed to multiply overnight."

"In all fairness, that's because—" He stopped with the look Harper gave him.

"And this is all while trying to figure out how I'm supposed to handle seeing..." She shook her head. "Never mind. It doesn't matter. But to answer your question: no, I have no idea what I'm going to do."

Austin looked back down at his clipboard, even though he'd memorized everything on it the night before. It was easier to stare at the words on the page than look into Harper's scrutinizing gaze.

"Who else knows she's missing besides us?" he asked, keeping his eyes on the notes in front of him.

"Besides us?" She paused just long enough for the word "us" to linger between them. "I told Sienna and Fox."

Austin managed to look back up at Harper and instantly regretted it. At some point, she'd gotten closer, or maybe the room just felt smaller the longer the two of them hid inside. But with their sudden proximity, he could see her face better than he had the last few days.

A couple of stray blond hairs framed her face, and the longer he stared, the softer her eyes became. They were the same gray eyes he'd stared into day after day in college, but the face around them had changed in the last four years.

There were the smallest lines forming in the corners, like her eyes were smiling even when her mouth wasn't. It was so unlike the botoxed starlets Austin was used to seeing. Even the production crew all seemed to get work done and spent hours obsessing over their weight and looks in an effort to fit in with the actresses. Harper's untouched face was a breath of fresh air he hadn't realized he needed.

"Austin?"

Her voice broke the trance, and he shook his head.

"Yeah, sorry." He cleared his throat. "So, um, can we trust Sienna and Fox not to say anything?"

We. Another one of those words that felt louder than the others. Or had he just said it louder? He needed to get out of this small room, and yet it was the only place he could actually talk to Harper without getting in trouble.

Harper nodded. "Yeah. Sienna is a little over the top, but she knows that we can't have any other problems. And Fox, well, he's as loyal as they come."

Loyal. Everything Austin wasn't. "Okay. That's good." He nodded. "But we still need to figure out what to do about Audrey. This is supposed to be dress day."

Harper bit her bottom lip. "And what exactly is supposed to happen on dress day?"

Austin looked back down at the clipboard—again. "The bridesmaids won the table decorating contest, so you're supposed to go dress shopping at a couple of boutiques today. Audrey has to be there."

A small sound of frustration came from Harper. "Well, she won't be. Isn't there anything you can do? You're a production assistant, right? Can you stall?"

Austin shook his head. "I can't."

"But you're a part of this whole crazy show."

Austin sighed. He really didn't want to admit how little power he had, but they were running out of time. Eventually, someone would come looking for him, or Harper—or both. And it would be bad news for everyone if they got caught together, especially in the safe room.

He took a deep breath. "Most days, I'm little more than a glorified coffee guy. Trust me when I say there is literally nothing I can do."

Harper stared at him for a moment before she nodded. "Okay, but even so, you've got to know a believable reason for Audrey to be missing."

He didn't.

The two stood in silence, both frantically trying to come up with an excuse. The seconds seemed to drag on until they both looked at each other and said at the same time, "We can pretend she's sick."

It felt like old times, when they would constantly say the same thing at the same time, or finish each other's sentences. Austin couldn't count how many times his college girlfriends would get jealous of his and Harper's friendship and the way they were always in tune with one another.

Austin and Harper laughed, but it only lasted a minute before they both seemed to realize that this wasn't like old times. Things had changed. By some unspoken cue, they both sobered.

Harper played with the hem of her shirt. "So, we pretend Audrey's sick. How do we do this?"

"I don't know. I can go talk to Bruce and let him know she's been throwing up all morning."

Harper's face scrunched up. "Does it have to be something so unflattering?"

"If it's just a stuffy nose, he's going to tell her to take some cold medicine and suck it up. Even with this, I can't promise he won't shove a bottle of the pink stuff in my hand and tell me to give it to her."

"Okay." Her eyes went to the ground. "Well, thank you."

"You're welcome."

Harper's eyes met his. "So what do we do now?"

Now?

Now, Austin wanted to explain why he'd left without saying goodbye and apologize for hurting her. But he knew he couldn't. Not with his entire career and her sister's wedding hanging in the balance.

"I'm going to have you go out first. See if there are any cameramen or other crew members in the hall. If not, knock on the door three times, and I'll know it's safe. You go find Sienna and Fox, and explain to them what's going on. And I'll go find Bruce."

Harper nodded. "And if there's someone out there?"

"Don't knock."

She took a breath, her annoyance barely contained. "What if it's someone from the wedding party looking to take a break in the safe room?"

Austin wasn't sure. Harper had said Sienna and Fox were trustworthy, and he wanted to believe her. But what about the other contestants? He didn't know much about Harper's family other than what she'd told him ages ago and what he'd seen. Mostly just the normal kind of family drama, though that Harry guy seemed like a real jerk.

He met her gaze. "Let's just hope that the coast is clear."

Harper agreed and slowly opened the door to the safe room. She peeked out the door, and Austin wanted to yell at her to just act casual but was afraid that if anyone was in the hall, they'd recognize his voice.

Mercifully, Harper finally walked into the hall and closed the door behind her. But once he was alone, time seemed to stretch on. Austin held his breath for what felt like an eternity as he waited for the knocks to come.

Eventually, they did.

He let out a relieved sigh and walked out. Harper was already walking left, not bothering to look back at him over her shoulder. And that was good. It was better than good. That meant she was taking Audrey's disappearance seriously.

With a tug at his heart, he watched Harper walk away for the briefest moment before he turned and walked in the opposite direction in search of Bruce.

THREE

5 Days Until Dream Wedding

HARPER'S good luck with the cameras had finally run out. On her way to find Sienna and Fox, she passed three roaming the halls on their way to set up for the first shot of the day. Harper checked her watch. Only thirty minutes until everyone was supposed to be in the meeting room. Hopefully that would be enough time to come up with some sort of plan.

Harper shook her head. Of course it was enough time for a plan. She could make three dozen cookies in thirty minutes, this should be easy. Or at least, it would be easy if the picture of Austin's frown wasn't stuck in her mind.

It was unfair how good he looked. California was clearly where Austin was supposed to be. He was probably on the beach every weekend, surrounded by beautiful starlets drooling all over him just like her roommates used to in college.

It was amazing how all the work she'd done over the last four years had been undone within moments of seeing Austin. She felt like the same inadequate girl from college—the too curvy, not pretty enough friend who happened to be a girl. Never the girlfriend.

Being trapped in the safe room tested her in unbearable ways. It took all her willpower to stay focused on Audrey's disappearance when there were so many other questions bouncing around in her mind.

Harper had wanted to ask him why he left. Why he never called. She wanted to know what he'd thought of all the awful superhero movies that had come out in the past year. She wondered if his arms still felt the same wrapped around her as they did when they were friends.

No, thinking about her ex-best friend would only distract her from what she needed to do. She laid it out step by step in her mind, like creating a new recipe. If she followed the recipe, nothing could go wrong.

Step 1: Find Fox and Sienna.

Step 2: Tell them that, as far as anyone knew, Audrey was sick in her room.

Step 3: Try not to get caught as she went around trying to find the bride.

Easy as pie, right?

It should have been, but even with a plan in place, Harper's heart raced as she ran up the stairs of the inn. She stopped to catch her breath when she reached the top.

She took a moment to admire the artwork that covered the walls. The owners had bought a lot from local talent and maybe the bakery could use some art. Harper shook her head. This always happened. She'd get halfway through something and get distracted. Things always got done eventually, but she couldn't linger. Not today. She had a wedding and a reality show to save. With thoughts of a furious producer racing in her mind, she barreled down the hallway, turned a corner and ran right into Sienna and Fox coming in the opposite direction.

"There you are!" Her younger sister barely stopped in time, saving the two girls from an embarrassing collision.

Harper sucked in a deep breath. "Sorry. I've been running around trying to figure out what to do."

Sienna threw up her hands. "And? What *are* we going to do?"

"Shh! Not here." Harper cast a glance back over her shoulder then dragged Sienna further down the hall and into her room.

It was ridiculous to have to stay at The Emerald Inn when Harper had a perfectly good apartment in town, but it was nice to not worry about cleaning or cooking for a few days. Despite the state of her own bedroom, Harper loved a tidy room. She just didn't have the time or energy to do it herself. Harper couldn't help but smile and breathe in deeply as she pushed her sister into her hotel room. Fox was close on their heels, and as soon as he was inside, Harper shut the door and leaned against it.

"Have you seen anyone else this morning?" Harper spoke quietly.

The hall behind the door was empty but it wouldn't stay like that for long. Plus the rooms weren't off limits for filming. Nothing was, except the safe room and the bathrooms. Assuming they didn't get caught, this would be their only chance at a covert planning session without drawing attention from the production crew.

Sienna shook her head. "We came back up here to

look for her, but didn't pass anyone. I think they're all in the dining hall or meeting room already."

"Why did you look? I already told you she wasn't here."

Sienna's cheeks went bright red. "I-uh-we…"

Harper couldn't figure out what had caused her sister to turn into a stammering idiot, until her eyes turned to Fox. He didn't say anything, but his matching blush was all the explanation Harper needed.

Harper exhaled slowly through her nose. The meeting room was surely packed with crew members by now. The brand new couple was just killing two birds with one stone. Looking for Audrey while enjoying a few stolen moments away from the cameras.

Not that Harper could blame them. She'd just had a stolen moment of her own with Austin, hadn't she? She ignored the tug at her heart reminding her it wasn't the same thing. Austin had never been hers. And besides, Harper was over him, and totally focused on solving the major crisis at hand.

So why was her heart racing at the thought of his amber eyes gazing into hers in the safe room?

Fox cleared his throat. "We thought maybe Audrey left a note somewhere." He glanced at Sienna.

Harper tried not to roll her eyes. She'd already searched and knew there wasn't a note.

"We tried calling, too, but it went right to voice-mail," Sienna said, sitting on the chair by the window. The light caught her perfect honey blond waves as she shook them off of her shoulders.

Harper's hand moved to the messy knot on top of her head. If she'd known she would be trapped in the safe room with Austin this morning she might have done something more than throw it up in her usual haphazard way.

Audrey. Finding Audrey. That's what Harper needed to think about right now. Not her hair. Not Austin.

Sienna looked up at her with wide eyes. "Do you think something bad happened to her?"

"I'm sure she's just gone somewhere to get a little peace." Harper sounded much more certain than she felt. "We've all been feeling totally cooped up."

Fox gave a soft "no kidding" and went to stand behind Sienna to lay a protective hand on her shoulder.

Sienna shook her head. "But we can't afford anymore screw-ups. She knows that. What are we going to do?"

"We'll find her," Fox said, his voice calm.

Sienna smiled adoringly up at Fox. Harper felt like an intruder to a private moment from her position leaning against the door.

Harper cleared her throat. "Austin's going to tell Bruce that Audrey is sick."

"Who's Austin?" Sienna's brows drew together.

With a churning twist of her stomach, Harper realized her mistake.

"Oh, just the production assistant who was there this morning," said Harper, wiping her clammy hands on her jeans. "His name was on his badge, remember?"

"Sure. Okay." Sienna nodded, but clearly didn't remember. She only had eyes for Fox this morning.

"He overheard us talking, so I had to tell him what was going on. But I told him I'd get her back here by tonight, and we just needed some time."

"Are you sure we can trust him?" asked Fox, his lips

twisted down in a frown. "He works for the show. For Bruce. This could all be a set up."

The words echoed Austin's question about Fox and Sienna. Why was everyone so suspicious of everyone else? And why were they all relying on Harper and her judge of character? She was far from the expert, given her history with her friends and family. She'd thought Austin would always stand by her. And Milo, her big brother. They'd both left her, and it had been a total shock each time.

But, in her gut, the same one that could tell a burned cookie from half a mile away, she knew that she could trust Austin with this secret.

"I trust him." Her words came out strong, without hesitation. Sienna's eyebrows shot up, but before she could open her mouth to inquire further, Harper pushed on. "But you may need to hang out in her room, to fend off anyone else who comes looking for her."

"And how exactly are we supposed to do that? Just because Audrey is feeling under the weather doesn't make her impossible to find," Sienna said.

"She'd need to be more than a little sick." Harper lifted a shoulder. "Austin is going to tell Bruce that she's throwing up."

"And what? Fox hides in the bathroom and makes sick noises while I fend off cameramen?"

Harper bit her bottom lip and looked at Fox. "If you wouldn't mind?"

He sighed and rubbed his hands through his hair. "I don't know. I mean, I'd do anything for Audrey and Eli and...Sienna." He looked down and smiled. Harper tried to keep the yearning she felt deep in her bones for a relationship of her own under control. "But won't they start wondering where I am? And why Sienna and I are apart after what happened last night?"

"Well, that would be the second part of my plan." Harper pushed off against the door. "We need to provide a distraction."

The solution to everything that suddenly came to mind involved using the newfound love between the best man and her little sister to their advantage. Harper hated that it would make Sienna look bad, especially after all the crap Audrey and Harper had given her about being too dramatic this week, but what other choice did they have?

Harper took a deep breath and held it for a moment. "I think you two should get into a really big fight," she said looking between Sienna and Fox.

Sienna shot up out of her seat. "No way. No more pretending."

"We don't really have a ton of options right now." Harper twisted her hands together. "We can all say Audrey is barfing her guts out, and you can make it sound convincing for a while, but then what are they supposed to film all day? We need to give them something good."

"But after everything Fox did yesterday, will they really believe it?" Sienna put her hand in his, turning her wide blue eyes up at him. Fox's on-camera declaration of love had been perfect. The kind Harper had been hoping for her entire life and knew she'd never get.

And, of course, Sienna made a great point. Harper wasn't sure the production staff—or, more importantly, Bruce—would believe these two were anything but gaga over each other.

Fox looked down at his honeybun, the words "no way" etched all over his face.

That couldn't happen. Harper needed them to get with the program until they could find Audrey. After that, she didn't care what the two of them did in their happily ever after.

"Are you not a good enough actress to make everyone think you hate him?" Harper said.

Sienna's nostrils flared, and Harper felt a surge of success. The sisters were nothing if not super competitive. She'd thrown out the challenge, and now Sienna would have to accept.

"It'll mean Fox needs to be on camera a lot, though." Sienna looked up at him, her eyes soft. "I know you don't want that."

Fox closed his eyes and sat down in the chair, head in his hands.

Harper held her breath. She knew Sienna could do it, but it took two to make an epic, fake fight believable.

Finally, Fox looked up and opened his eyes. "I'm here to make sure Eli and Audrey get the dream wedding they want and deserve. If that means pretending to lose my breakfast and throwing a hissy fit for the camera then well…" He shrugged. "I guess that's what I'll have to do."

Sienna threw her arms around him, and Harper was tempted to rush across the room to do the same. This guy was everything Sienna needed. Loyal and generous.

Basically the opposite of all the men in Harper's life.

"What are you going to do while we're busy battling it out?" Sienna asked, her arms still around Fox's shoulders.

Harper shrugged. "I'm the only one allowed to leave

the property, so I'll go look in town, at her house." Technically that was true. She was allowed with permission from the producer, but Harper didn't have any intention of letting him know about this trip.

"Won't the cameras follow you?" Fox asked. "It's not like you can just go around town unnoticed. They were there the other night at the bakery."

"They were until someone caused a distraction to pull them away," Harper said with a quirk of a smile as she remembered the way the cameraman raced out of her bakery like she'd set something on fire. That fire, of course, had been Fox and the rest of the guys running through town like a bunch of frat boys during initiation. "If you and Wade escaping the inn was enough to pull all the cameras away to look for you, then I'm sure whatever you and Sienna pull off will keep them occupied."

Sienna frowned. "Are you sure?"

Harper pursed her lips to keep from letting out a frustrated sigh. "Trust me. I'll figure this out."

She had to. There was no other option.

FOUR

5 Days Until Dream Wedding

AUSTIN DEBATED who he should tell first about Audrey's "illness."

The answer should have been obvious, but it was the one that made his stomach twist more than it did while with Harper in the safe room. He had to tell Bruce and hope that the producer didn't lash out at the messenger.

A runaway bride isn't your fault, he told himself. So why did it feel like this was strike two of the universe versus Austin? He'd gotten his feelings for Harper under control. Mostly. But now he had to explain to his boss that the entire schedule for the day had to be scrapped.

This was going to be rough.

Austin found Bruce near the equipment tent. He was surrounded by a lot of tired faces staring into space. This show was just one unexpected twist after another.

"Let's get in there, fifteen minutes everyone," Bruce called out, and everyone scurried into action.

"Um, Mr. Bigg?" Austin wondered, not for the first time, if that was really Bruce's last name.

The producer whirled to look at Austin, his eyes taking him in.

Austin swallowed hard but didn't lower his gaze under Bruce's scrutiny. "I think the bride may be out of commission today."

There was a pause, and Austin worried his thumping heart would give the game away.

"What on earth does that mean?" Bruce crossed his arms over his wide chest and raised one thick eyebrow.

Austin took a deep breath of the fresh mountain air. The earthy, wet smell of freshly cut grass calmed his racing heart to a reasonable pace. "She's sick. Really sick. I ran into one of the sisters this morning and apparently she's been puking up her guts all night. I don't think anyone will be trying on dresses today."

Bruce smiled slowly, a slick and cold movement of his lips that gave Austin a chill. He was the Grinch plotting to take Christmas away from all the Whos in Whoville. "Don't worry about it. I have a plan."

Of course he did. Bruce was a professional and would make sure the show ran smoothly.

It was why he was one of the best reality show producers in the business, and Austin had so much to learn from him. Of course, he was also demanding and a perfectionist and didn't really care about how much work he piled on others. But what producer wasn't like that? Austin had been doing this for a few years and had just accepted that's how it was. Just like he'd accepted that he'd be getting coffee for at least another few years before he'd be able to move up in the food chain.

But this was his chance. Getting this gig had been totally last minute and was a step above what he'd been doing before. And Bruce had so many connections that this job would be his launching pad into something even better.

Austin perked up as Bruce launched into the crew's new plan.

"We have five days until the wedding. And we've got a lot to squeeze into those days. So don't think we're going to have an off day just because the bride is hungover." Bruce flashed a smug smile at everyone, earning a few soft chuckles.

Austin opened his mouth to argue that alcohol wasn't the problem. But he didn't actually know Audrey beyond what he'd seen so far this week. And he most certainly wasn't supposed to know Harper, or any of the contestants for that matter. So he clamped his lips together and let everyone continue to think it was a case of Audrey struggling to hold her liquor.

"We got group interviews our first day of filming, but now that we have the competitions under our belts, we can get some individual shots with everyone. Ask them what was going through their head for each one."

Austin felt his shoulders relax. That was doable.

"Not to mention, Fox and Sienna still owe me a joint interview after they practically shut down production with their little stunts."

That could work to his advantage too. They were the only other people who really knew what was going on, and if Austin could get assigned to them, it might give him an opportunity to stay one step ahead of this mess.

But first, he needed to get his head back in the game. He'd been making mistakes all week, totally off his A-game, thanks to his constant awareness of where Harper was. A gust of wind brought the scent of cinnamon over from the inn, and the steely gray of Harper's eyes popped into Austin's mind.

He had to get this under control, and stat, if he had any hope of getting through the next five days with his job—and his heart—intact.

The bustle of the tent was a good distraction, and he threw himself into work. Changing the plan for the day meant different supplies, calling to cancel the dress appointment, and a hundred other tasks. Noting them all down and crossing them off gave back Austin the sense of control he so desperately needed.

Just as he got off the phone with a vendor to arrange for them to arrive the following day instead, Jennifer, the other production assistant, walked in and made a beeline for him. Her crush on him was frustrating enough on a normal day, but he absolutely couldn't handle her hanging on his every word right now. Her usual cheery smile and playful attitude were missing, however, when she stormed over. Austin's pulse raced at the sight of her serious face.

She knows something's up.

No, Austin was just being paranoid like a child who snuck a cookie before dinner and was afraid of getting caught. Not that he should be thinking about cookies right now.

"I just went to check on the bride, as commanded," Jennifer said, and leaned both hands on the table where Austin was sitting.

"How's she doing?" He tried to keep his face completely blank, but had the feeling it looked more like he was about to hurl.

Jennifer raised an eyebrow. "I only heard through

the crack in the door when Sienna poked her head out, but she sounded terrible."

"Yeah that's what I heard too."

"You saw Sienna this morning?"

"Uh no, the other sister, Harper."

"Oh, when did you see Harper? I haven't seen her yet today."

Crap, he should have just said it was Sienna. Austin could feel the sweat start to pool under his arms. "Just before breakfast. I ran into her in the hall."

"And you haven't seen her since?"

"Uh, no. Look, Jennifer, I still have a lot of calls to make. You know how Bruce is when things don't go how he wants them to, so I'd better get to it."

She looked him up and down, then smiled wide and fluttered her lashes a little. "Right, I totally get it. Bruce seems to really trust you with all the important stuff."

Austin's stomach twisted, but he managed a smile and a nod. He stood up and turned to head out the door.

"Just one more thing." She moved in front of him and bit her lip. "I didn't mention it before, when I was doing my research, because I didn't want to make something out of nothing, but I noticed Harper went to the same college you did. Graduated the same year."

"Okay." He struggled to keep his voice even.

"And with everything else, I have to ask." She leaned in close and whispered, "You didn't know her, did you?"

Austin sucked in a breath, unsure how to answer. Jennifer might see through a lie, and she may already know the answer considering her "research." If she suspected Austin was being dishonest, it would put tension between them, and he needed Jennifer on his side for whatever was going to happen today.

Austin had planned for a lot, but had never expected this.

"I knew her, sort of, but I haven't seen her or talked to her since graduation." He didn't add that it was because he'd broken her heart. Jennifer didn't need to know he'd been too embarrassed to crawl back to Harper and beg for forgiveness about three seconds later when he'd realized what a horrible mistake he'd made.

"You need to disclose if you've had a previous relationship with anyone in the cast," Jennifer said, looking a little panicked. "You know Bruce's rules. No external contact with the cast. You'll get fired."

She managed to look much more upset about that prospect than Austin did. He waved away her concerns. "It was *not* a relationship."

Jennifer put her hand on his shoulder and squeezed it. "You can tell me, I won't tell anyone, I promise. I just need to know in case anyone else spots what I did."

"We just had some mutual friends during college. It's no big deal. Really." Austin moved away from her hand and headed toward the door again, hoping she couldn't see the lie written across his face. "And I also really need to make these calls."

"Okay," Jennifer called out after him. "But let me know if I can help with anything. You can trust me."

What was it about everyone and their trust? First, it was Harper reassuring Austin that he could trust Fox and Sienna. Now, Jennifer was telling him to trust her. Who could really keep his secrets when it mattered?

Out in the morning sun, he inhaled deeply, willing his mind to calm. Control slowly fell back into place. His gut told him he couldn't trust Jennifer, the girl he'd worked with on countless sets. But he knew in his heart he'd follow Harper to the ends of the earth. And if Harper vouched for Fox and Sienna, then that meant he would put his trust in them too.

He let out a breath, relieved to have at least one thing settled. But his mind continued to race about his conversation with Jennifer. Why on earth was she bringing this up now, five days into filming? Had she noticed Austin talking to Harper in the hall earlier?

He knew Jennifer liked him, but he hadn't thought it reached stalker proportions already. Usually girls got the hint after politely saying "no" two or three times to their invitations to happy hour. Jennifer was particularly persistent, but also a great colleague to have on set with him. Almost as organized as he was.

Austin made his way into the open space beside the parking lot, but wished he could escape to the trees. He had his walkie-talkie, so he was reachable if Bruce needed him, but Austin liked to stay in sight of Bruce whenever possible. Just in case there was some random task to be done, he'd be the first person Bruce would see. For the first time in his career, Austin wanted to disappear. Would anyone besides Jennifer even notice?

Disappearing was what he did best, wasn't it?

He hadn't been lying when he told Jennifer that he needed to make some calls for Bruce. He wandered a few yards into the wooded area, letting himself pretend he could disappear while he did so. He could feel the weight of the walkie-talkie on his hip, and the pressure of making sure all of the vendors he was responsible for knew what to do.

When Austin finished up the last of his phone calls,

he stepped back out into the clearing and turned to head back to the inn. Since the new plan was to get individual interviews with everyone in the family, it would mean lots of standing around and waiting. Austin normally liked the mindless calm of days like that, but today he was antsy and needed to move around.

He checked his watch. It was digital and displayed the time down to a tenth of a second. He'd had it for years, and could remember Harper making fun of it the first time he'd worn it. "No one wears a watch like that except super nerds. Girls won't go out with you if you wear that."

If only she'd been right, then maybe things would have turned out differently.

The giant, green, blinking numbers told him he had exactly thirteen minutes until he had to be somewhere. Just enough time to a loop around the perimeter. And maybe he'd spot a sign of the runaway bride while he was getting his recommended dose of vitamin D for the day.

Three seconds into his walk, however, a movement in the parking lot caught his eye. Hope swelled in his chest.

But it wasn't Audrey, back with a tale of wedding nerves or engine trouble. It was Harper, sneaking through the cars, casting covert looks over her shoulder every few feet to be sure she wasn't being followed.

When she caught Austin's eye, the color drained out of her face.

Harper was up to something, and Austin needed to know what it was.

5 Days Until Dream Wedding

HARPER CROUCHED between two cars while she waited for the inevitable. As sneaky as she'd tried to be, Austin had caught her trying to make her escape. It wasn't fair after she'd worked so hard to get Sienna and Fox to do what she needed in order to go downtown.

But it wasn't like she could make a run for it now.

The seconds dragged on as Harper stayed hidden. Her thighs started to burn from holding her position for so long. She was about to say screw it and stand up when Austin finally ducked behind the car.

"What are you doing?" he whispered harshly.

"What do you think I'm doing? I'm trying to find Audrey."

He lifted a brow. "And you think she's hiding under one of these cars?"

"Yep. Totally. If only I would have looked under this Jeep *before* freaking out and jumping to conclusions." She shook her head. "No, of course not. I'm sneaking downtown to see if I can find her there. Or at least, I *was* until you saw me."

"Do you think she's there?"

Her muscles continued to burn, and Harper really wished she would have bolted when she had the chance. That, or find someplace she could stand or lean more comfortably. The pain made her irritable on top of everything else that was going on. Her arms could carry two giant hot metal trays at once without even a quiver. But her buns were more like actual buns than anything even close to resembling steel.

"I don't know," she snapped, forgetting to keep her voice low. She held her breath for a few seconds to see if anyone heard her. When things seemed safe, she tried again, her voice softer. "I thought I could check out her apartment, and then mine."

Austin scrunched his eyebrows together. "Why would she be in your apartment?"

"Who knows? Maybe she needed a de-stressing snuggle with Mister Mittens."

Austin blinked a few times, and Harper's cheeks heated. "That would be my cat." Who she really wished had a much less dorky name right about now.

He cleared his throat. "Right. And I assume Bruce did not approve this little excursion?"

Ugh, four years later and Austin was still such a stickler for the rules. Harper avoided meeting his eyes. "That would not be an incorrect assumption."

He sighed. "What did you plan to do if you get caught?"

"I wasn't planning on it."

He leaned in close, and Harper could smell his cologne. It was the same scent he'd always worn in college—the one she'd gotten him for Christmas one year as a joke—and with every inhale came a flood of butterflies and memories. "I hate to break it to you, but you've already been caught."

She scoffed. "By you? That doesn't count."

Austin grabbed her arm and looked her in the eye. "I'm being serious. What would you say to Bruce, or anyone else, if they saw you playing *James Bond* through the parking lot?"

Harper felt her temper flare with Austin's never ending questions. She shrugged off his hand. "I'd tell them I was going to Flour Girl. One of the perks of being a business owner."

Austin's face softened. "I think it's really great that you've started it, by the way. I ate some of the pastries you left for the crew the other day. I don't think I've ever had an éclair that was so delicious."

A delicious rush of pride ran through Harper's veins. "Thanks. I—"

The sound of footsteps made Harper stop short. Her eyes went wide, and she could hear Austin's sharp inhale from where he was still crouched beside her. The car next to the one they were hiding behind started up and they let out a collective whoosh of relief. It hadn't given their position away, but they couldn't stay here indefinitely.

Harper was going to be sore tomorrow from staying in this position for so long. She nearly wept in gratitude when he started wagging his finger between the two of them and pointed to a large hedge a few yards away—a hedge that she could actually stand behind.

She nodded, and Austin snuck a look in the direction of The Emerald Inn. "Okay, the coast is clear. One...two..."

Harper didn't wait for three. With a quick look of

her own toward the inn, she hopped up and started jogging over to the hedge. She was so relieved to be finally standing, she practically moaned.

Seconds later, Austin was standing beside her, his amber eyes stormy. "You were supposed to wait for me to say three."

"Nobody was looking."

He put his hands on his hips. "What if they were?"

"Then saying the word three wasn't going to change anything."

Austin let out a deep sigh and pinched the bridge of his nose. It was a look Harper knew well, and her heart did a little somersault at the familiarity of it. He opened one eye and glared at her. "You're not going to make this easy, are you?"

"None of this is easy. But Audrey made up her mind to get married this way, so what choice do I have?"

"You're really close to her now." It wasn't a question. Austin had his eyes open now, and was looking at Harper with his eyebrows scrunched up. "You weren't before."

Harper ran her hands along the leaves of the bush. "Yeah, well, things change."

His cheeks turned slightly pink, but he didn't say anything. She hadn't needed to be close to her sisters in college because she'd had Austin. He must know what huge a hole it had left in her when he left. But given his radio silence since graduation, he just didn't care.

"Anyway, thanks for helping me out back there." Harper looked down at her feet, unable to keep eye contact with Austin. "I'll try to cover as much ground as I possibly can in an hour or two, and will try to find you when I get back."

Harper turned on her heel to make her way down the mountain, anxious to get away from Austin, and the painful memories that resurfaced whenever he was near her.

"Aren't you going to get your car?" Austin asked.

Harper kept walking and didn't look back. "Audrey's car is already missing. I don't want someone to notice another one gone."

"So you're walking all the way to town?"

Harper sighed and stopped, hands on her hips and eyes looking skyward. "Just to the highway, then I'll get a rideshare."

There was the crunch of leaves and gravel behind her then a strong hand grabbed her arm and held her back. "You're not going alone."

Harper shook off Austin's hand and whirled to face him. "Of course I am."

"I'm coming with you."

"You most certainly are not."

Austin stepped closer. "You need my help."

She shook her head. "I can do this on my own."

A corner of his mouth lifted in the stupid grin that used to drive her crazy. "Just like you passed Italian on your own?"

"Last time I checked, conjugating verbs isn't the same as finding a missing bride before the producer finds out."

"And it's not smart for you to be out alone."

Harper crossed her arms over her chest. "You mean in *my* hometown?"

"I mean, with *Wedding Games*. Besides, I think we should keep looking here first before you go trooping through town."

"Trooping?" Harper lifted her brow.

"You know what I mean."

She rolled her eyes. "Yeah, and I told you, I already searched everywhere at the hotel."

"But you didn't."

Harper balled her hands into fists. He was the same know-it-all he'd always been. It was one thing to show off in college in front of sorority girls or help Harper with her Italian. But now he wanted to crash back into her life four years later, in Wellspring of all places, and act like he knew this place better than Harper? That wasn't happening.

She straightened her shoulders. "But I did."

"Hear me out." Austin held up his hands. "I had to canvas the entire property on my first day to look for places that people might try to sneak off to. At first, I thought Bruce was crazy. But I couldn't tell you how many hidden nooks and crannies I found."

Harper felt her certainty dissolve. He may actually have something to offer her in this situation. Not that she wanted to admit it.

"Fine. But if we don't find her in any of your secret hideouts, I'm going downtown. And you're not going to stop me. Do you understand?"

Austin nodded.

"Then lead the way."

SIX

5 Days Until Dream Wedding

AUSTIN RESISTED the urge to grab Harper's hand as they headed back to The Emerald Inn. In college, they had shared an easy friendship that made wrapping their arms around each other as natural as breathing. But they weren't in college anymore, and he wasn't sure how she would react after all these years. Austin wanted to think the friendship they'd had was still there under her hard exterior, but that was a fantasy even bigger than gender equality in Hollywood.

He could see the anger simmering just below the surface every time he opened his mouth. And he'd noticed the way her hands curled into fists when they argued. It would have been cute if she wasn't legitimately angry with him.

Not that any of this was his fault—at least, not the current predicament they found themselves in. The Hudson sisters were giving all the drama Bruce could ever ask for, but it was Austin who would have to clean it up. The least she could do was listen to him and let him help.

No, that wasn't fair to Harper. He'd been the one who burned that bridge—not her. And now he had to deal with the consequences.

Thankfully, Austin already had his clipboard with him so that if the two of them were caught together, it would look like they were doing something show-related. Unless Jennifer caught them.

Austin couldn't let that happen.

On the first day of filming, Bruce had laid out some serious consequences for fraternizing with the contestants of *Wedding Games,* and all production staff were encouraged to speak as little as possible with them. Most people didn't need to be told twice. The threat of being fired, and possibly blacklisted, was enough motivation for most people to treat the contestants like they had the plague.

Austin held his show notes in front of him as Harper followed him through the halls of The Emerald Inn. And to her credit, she didn't argue or make any sarcastic comments. They passed a few hotel staff and a lone cameraman rushing to get to wherever Bruce had commanded him to go. Austin glanced down at the schedule. Eli's interview was up first.

Once the hallway was clear, Harper jogged up so she was beside Austin, instead of trailing him. He ignored the sudden drop in his stomach at her proximity. A hint of cinnamon and vanilla wafted off of her.

What did she do, bathe in everything delicious?

"What did Bruce say when you told him Audrey was sick?" she asked.

Austin shrugged. "He already had a new plan in place."

"Which is?"

Right. Of course she'd want to know. And even though Austin knew he shouldn't be sharing information with Harper—Bruce liked his cast to be kept in the dark as much as possible—she'd find out eventually. And Austin was already breaking so many other rules just by being on set with her.

"He's doing individual interviews with everyone. And also decided this was the perfect day to cash in on the deal he made with Fox and Sienna."

"What deal?"

"He gets a joint interview in exchange for all of yesterday's craziness."

Harper stopped, and when Austin turned to see what was going on, her face had gone completely pale.

With two quick steps, he closed the distance between them. But Harper stood rooted in place, her gaze on the floor. When she refused to meet his eyes, Austin reached out and touched her arm. "What's wrong?"

She shook her head, but kept her eyes downcast. "They're both in Audrey's room covering for her. Fox is pretending to throw up in the bathroom if anyone comes by."

"Oh crap."

"Oh crap is right." She looked up, her eyes wide. "Do you know who's supposed to interview them? Or when?"

Austin looked down at his notes: Jennifer. And not for a few hours.

"We're good for now. But the sooner we can find Audrey, the better."

Harper nodded. "Okay," she said, but her teeth tugged at her lower lip.

This time, Austin didn't stop his hand from grabbing

Harper's. He reached out and intertwined his fingers with hers. With a squeeze, he said, "It's going to be okay."

"You don't know that." She looked down at his hand but didn't pull away.

Austin's heart skipped a beat. "You're right. But that doesn't mean we have to give up. We can start with some of the employee areas. There's the kitchen, the maid stations, and a few closets that aren't being used. From there, we can check some of the outside areas, including the barn."

She gave him the tiniest smile that sent his heart thumping so hard, she was sure to hear it. But as much as he wanted to savor every moment of their intimate contact, he couldn't risk getting caught by a member of the crew who might happen to be roaming the same halls as they were.

He released her hand, immediately missing its warmth, and led them to the kitchen. While the production staff was given free rein over most of the property, it was one of the few places everyone—including the cast—weren't allowed to go.

The first day of filming, the head chef had insisted she meet with the crew of *Wedding Games* to explain that the room was off limits, even though Bruce had written that into the contract with the owners. Marcey rattled on about food safety and the health department and not wanting her secrets shown on national television. She had made it very clear that, even though the owners of The Emerald Inn had agreed to the filming, she was still the boss of her domain.

But even the head chef had to take a break sometimes, and Austin hoped that time was now. She was only serving the cast and crew of the show, so that had to mean less work than usual. He paused by the door and took a deep breath. It would only take a minute to peek inside and see if Audrey was hiding there. But Austin did not want to upset the person in charge of feeding them all.

"Are we going inside?" Harper asked.

He cleared his throat. "Yep, just waiting for you."

Harper rolled her eyes and pushed her way past Austin so that she walked through the door first. And then immediately stopped.

"Is she there?" Austin asked, craning his neck to look around Harper.

She shook her head, her back still to him.

"Then what's going on?"

"It's beautiful," she whispered as she took a couple of steps inside the room.

Austin walked in behind her, and saw a normal kitchen. "Uh, what are you talking about?"

She twirled to face him, and the smile on her face took his breath away. "This." She held up her hands and waved them around. "Marcey's never let me in here before, not even when I made an emergency cake for a big wedding last year."

Austin shook his head. "Still not following you. It's just a kitchen." He glanced at his watch. They'd been in here more than a minute, and he didn't want to linger when there was a bride to find and a cranky chef who could pop in at any moment.

"Just a kitchen?" She held a hand to her heart in shock. "Look at all this space. There are three ovens, a gas stovetop—" She gasped. "Is that a Hobart Legacy?"

"Uh..."

She walked over to a large mixer. "Would you look at it's triple interlock system and VFD?"

Austin had no clue what she was talking about. And again, it looked like a regular mixer to Austin—only bigger and with presumably more buttons than something you grabbed at Walmart. But the way Harper's face lit up as she ran her fingers along it made Austin realize it was something special.

Harper was something special, and he'd been an idiot.

She looked up at Austin. "In a perfect world, this is the mixer that I'd use at Flour Girl."

And in a perfect world, Austin would be the one to buy it for her.

But this wasn't a perfect world, and as much as Austin wanted to let Harper stay in the kitchen forever, the allotted few minutes of kitchen checking were up.

He bent his head over his clipboard and made a check mark on the list of places to check he'd made while they were walking back to the inn. "Well, it looks like she's not here. Let's go check out some of the other places on my list."

Harper shook her head. "Just another minute."

Austin's uneasy gaze went to the door and back. They were extremely lucky they hadn't been caught yet, and he didn't want to test their luck. "Harper."

"Hey, do you remember that time we studied all night and forgot to eat dinner?" She opened and closed some drawers, each one causing an envious expression to pass over her face.

While there were many times they'd stayed up late and had forgotten to go to the school's cafeteria before they closed for the night, there was only one night she meant. That night was permanently burned in his memory.

Austin nodded, even though Harper was still rummaging through Marcey's drawers. "Yeah. We were both freshmen, and neither one of us had missed dinner in the cafeteria before. And even though dinner had ended two hours earlier, we went down anyway."

Harper paused her investigation and looked at Austin. "You were hoping they left chips out."

"And alas, it was empty." He leaned against a counter. Once she got started with a story, she had to finish.

"But then I tried one of the doors, and it was unlocked. I couldn't believe it."

"And you were so excited." Austin still remembered the way her face lit up when she walked in and proceeded to make dinner for the two of them. The same shining eyes and excited smile were on her face now.

Until it shifted into a sad smile. "That was a fun night."

"It was."

It was the first time Austin had ever done anything like that in his life, and probably would have been the last, if it hadn't cemented their friendship. They'd shifted from classmates and dorm neighbors into something unbreakable.

Or almost unbreakable.

"Well, we should probably get going," Harper said.

"You mean before someone catches you sneaking in her kitchen?"

Their heads snapped in the direction of the stern, female voice.

Marcey stood in the doorway with her arms crossed. "Would either of you like to tell me what you're doing in my kitchen?" Her eyes narrowed at Austin. "Especially you. I know you were at that meeting."

Austin thought he might faint. "I, uh…"

Harper took a few steps toward Marcey and put out her hand. "Hi, I'm Harper Hudson."

Marcey kept her arms folded. "I know who you are. You made a cake for us last year. It was good."

Harper beamed. At least Marcey seemed to like someone involved in *Wedding Games*.

"You're that sassy one's older sister."

Or maybe not.

Harper chuckled nervously. "Yeah, Sienna is a little much."

Marcey lifted a brow.

Harper glanced at Austin for help, but he could barely breathe in and out.

"Anyway, as you know, I own Flour Girl Bakery downtown, and I just wanted to see your kitchen and…" Harper's words died off as Marcey continued to give her an icy stare.

Austin finally found his voice. "And I happened to be walking by and heard her. So, I came in to let her know she shouldn't be in here."

Marcey tilted her head ever so slightly.

"And now it's time for us to go," he said and grabbed Harper's hand and pulled her out of the kitchen.

They hurried down the hall, Austin's heart beating wildly as they put distance between them and the kitchen. But once they turned the corner, Austin and Harper both leaned against the wall, panting. Their eyes met and they both started laughing.

"Did you see the way she looked at you?" Austin said between fits of laughter.

Harper reached out and shoved his shoulder. "No thanks to you throwing me under the bus," she said, giggling.

"That's what you get for looking through every. Single. Drawer."

"You should have warned me she had such an amazing kitchen."

"Yeah, well, at the end, I was afraid she was going to put us in that Colbert Heritage you loved so much."

Harper's face suddenly went serious. "It's a Hobart Legacy. And we would never fit."

Austin looked at her with lowered brows. Was she really that serious about a mixer? Soon, the corners of her mouth twitched, and Harper was laughing hard again.

The moment was perfect, and Austin would have loved to stay in that hall with Harper for the rest of the day. But the staticky sound of Bruce's voice came from his walkie-talkie.

He barked out orders for Jennifer and some of the other crew before Austin heard his name.

"Austin."

He lifted the walkie-talkie to his mouth. "Sir?"

"I just wanted to check in with you and see how our changes are going."

Austin looked down at his clipboard. "Good. The boutique is able to accommodate Audrey and her sisters tomorrow, assuming she's feeling better. "

"And how is the bride?"

Harper's eyes went wide, and Austin tried to give her a reassuring smile before he cleared his throat. "I haven't been up to see her yet. Jennifer said she heard her puking her guts out."

There was a long pause, and Austin thought his heart might burst from his chest.

"Make sure to check on her at some point, and keep me posted."

"Yes, sir."

"And Austin?"

"Sir?"

"You're doing a great job keeping things from falling apart. I'm glad I can trust you."

A warm sense of pride filled Austin's chest, but was quickly snuffed out by the crush of guilt from lying to his boss. He glanced at Harper, who was frowning at him, and cleared his throat. "Thank you, sir."

He waited to see if Bruce would add anything else, but the walkie went quiet.

Harper sighed, leaned back against the wall, and closed her eyes.

Austin would have given anything to make her laugh again. But he was frozen, panic coursing through his veins. He couldn't let Harper do this on her own. Bruce would eat her alive. Yet the more time Austin spent with her, the more likely it was that he'd hurt her again. The secrets were piling up, and who knew when they'd come crashing down around him.

"Well," she said and turned to look at him, her gray eyes full of all the regret Austin held in his heart. "I guess we'd better keep looking."

SEVEN

5 Days Until Dream Wedding

OKAY, so getting caught in the kitchen with Austin had been kind of fun.

And before Bruce interrupted over the walkie-talkie, it almost felt like old times—getting caught doing something stupid together, laughing at their narrow escapes, holding hands...in a totally platonic way, of course.

The moment had been so perfect, Harper almost forgot the way he'd ripped her heart out. And now that the perfect moment was over, the pain was all she could think about. It was as fresh as it had been four years ago.

Austin had always been the cool guy. The gorgeous, funny guy. The one that girls flocked to at parties. The kind Harper would never have a shot with. But thanks to the randomness of freshman-year dorm room assignments, Harper and Austin had lived right across the hall from one another.

The two had become instant best friends the day he poked his head in her doorway to introduce himself. When he'd seen that Harper had a cheesy teen movie on, Austin plopped down next to her on her bed and started watching. They'd spent the next hour making commentary like they were on *Mystery Science Theater 3000.*

It was no wonder Harper had been a goner for Austin from that first meeting. But he'd been a goner for her much taller, thinner, and prettier roommate, Katrina, the instant she walked through the door.

And that was pretty much the story of Harper's life for the next four years. She was the kooky best friend, relegated to the role of funny sidekick. And, of course, confidant to Austin's love troubles as he worked through the Greek girls—all the way from Alpha to Omega.

But after years of pining after Austin, and seeing him choose the wrong girl time after time, Harper had decided enough was enough. They had just walked off the stage at graduation with diplomas and mortar boards in their hands as they waited for their friends to find them in the teeming mass of bodies. There had been nothing to lose by telling Austin how she felt. It would be like the end of one of those ridiculous rom-coms they loved to make fun of. At least, that's what she thought.

Harper could still remember the bile rising in her throat when his response to her big declaration was to turn on his heel and walk away. She could still remember the ache of her chest from crying every night for weeks when he'd cut off contact completely. She'd even stopped baking during those first horrible, lonely weeks. She would have been okay if all she'd done was completely blow any shot of a relationship out of the water, but it was so much worse than she could have ever expected. Harper had lost her best friend that day.

Their time in The Emerald Inn's kitchen didn't

change that. Austin had shown his true colors on graduation day, and Harper had moved on—really. Now she needed to keep her distance so she wouldn't get hurt again.

They were both quiet as she followed Austin through the rest of the inn, looking at the secret spots he'd told her about. There were fewer than he'd originally made it sound like, but it still took forever to check them all. Didn't his stupid, beautiful face know that every minute they spent together was torture for her?

Plus, avoiding all the crew members walking around was impossible. Twice someone stopped Austin to ask what he was doing, and each time, Harper's stomach closed up tight as a fist. Like this whole thing wasn't stressful enough.

They'd just finished searching the barn, when Austin let out a huge sigh. "Well, it looks like she really isn't here at the inn."

Harper sat down on one of the decorative bales of hay artfully arranged by the barn door. "I told you. Now, can I go down to the bakery?"

"Of course."

Harper hopped up.

"But I'm coming with you."

She rolled her eyes. "This again?" She put her hands on her hips. "Wellspring is my home, and Flour Girl is my business. I'm pretty sure I can handle it by myself."

Austin flashed her a wide grin. "I have no doubt that you can. You were always tough."

His words tugged at her heart—not to mention that smile—but she pushed the warm feelings down. She didn't have the ability to process this right now. Not when she was working so hard to keep her walls up. "So what's with the eagerness to come along? I'd have thought you have more important things to do."

Austin lifted up the walkie-talkie. "I just thought it might be helpful if I came since I have this. We can search for Audrey while getting to hear what's going on with the production staff, and most importantly, Bruce."

Harper hated that he made such an excellent point. She hated that she needed him, and she hated that she'd lost the argument. But she had bigger issues to deal with than her conflicting feelings about Austin. She needed to find Audrey before anyone found out she was missing.

"Fine. But I'm driving, and I get to pick the music."

The corner of his mouth lifted. "I wouldn't have it any other way."

They circled back around the inn toward the parking lot and, for once, luck was on their side. It was empty of any crew members or staff. The two hurried to Harper's station wagon.

"Wait," Austin said, his eyes wide with panic.

Harper's heart nearly stopped. She looked out the window of the car, searching for signs that they'd been spotted.

"Do you think driving is the best idea?" he asked, his mouth turned down. "Before you were ready to walk to the highway then rideshare."

Harper glared at him. "That was before someone wasted an hour looking at the inn where I already knew she wasn't." And before her legs had almost turned to pastry cream from crouching behind the car then walking all over the property.

"Let me just call it in so people don't get suspicious." He grabbed the walkie-talkie at his side before Harper could protest. It crackled to life, and he cycled through a few frequencies before finding the right one. "This is Austin. Harper needs to check on something at the bakery. She'll be back in time for her interview at one."

"She alone?" came the crackling response.

Austin glanced at Harper, and she shook her head. They couldn't know he was with her or then they'd really be suspicious.

"Affirmative."

"Thanks for the update. Get back in here to the mother's room, we need to redo a few shots."

"Sorry can you repeat? I'm out near the trees and —" He clicked off the walkie and dropped it in the backseat. "Whoops, looks like I just lost the connection."

Harper turned her wide eyes to him. "Did you seriously just do that?"

He nodded, but looked a little pale. "Let's just get this over quickly, okay?"

For the first time, Harper realized how much Austin was putting at risk to help her. His entire career was about to topple over like an over-baked soufflé, but he didn't seem to care about anything other than her sister. It was almost enough to make things up to her.

Almost.

She held her breath as she maneuvered her way out of the parking lot. Once The Emerald Inn disappeared behind the many trees that covered the side of the mountain, she finally breathed freely.

She snuck a glance in Austin's direction. "Looks like having an inside man came in handy."

He laughed. "Oh, yeah. Because that was some serious *Ocean's Eleven* stuff back there."

"It kind of feels like it. And Bruce can be that guy who owned the casino. What was his name?"

"I don't remember. But I can definitely see the comparison." He waggled his eyebrows at her. "Does that mean you're Julia Roberts' character?"

Harper bit back the snort that threatened to surface. "I guess that would make you George Clooney, the liar and thief that broke her heart." She'd meant it as a joke, but she couldn't hide the hurt in her voice.

Austin's smile vanished.

This wasn't a movie, and they weren't on the set of *Ocean's Eleven*. They were filming *Wedding Games*, sure to be one of the worst reality shows in history, Audrey was still missing, and even though they'd gotten Bruce's approval, there was no guarantee they'd be back before someone noticed the bride was nowhere on the premises. Hopefully Sienna and Fox would be able to keep everyone distracted with a fight of Julia Roberts and George Clooney proportions.

A tense silence hung between them as they drove into town. Form the corner of her eye, Harper could see Austin shift in his seat and open his mouth, as if he wasn't sure if he wanted to—what? Apologize for breaking her heart?

"Do you want to put on some music?" Austin asked hesitantly.

Harper bit her bottom lip. Yes. No. She didn't know. Being in such a confined space with Austin made it hard to know *what* she wanted.

She wanted things to go back to normal. She wanted to reach out and touch him. She wanted to slam on the breaks and kick him out of her car. She wanted her body to stop cataloging every little move-ment he made from the passenger seat as she pressed the gas pedal closer to the floorboard in an effort to get them to Flour Girl and out of this car as fast as possible.

"You drive a station wagon now," Austin said, not giving Harper the silence that she thought she wanted.

"And?"

"I never expected to see you in something like this. Not with the way you always talked about getting a bright-red convertible in school. I remember you had all those magazine cutouts on your 'dream board.'"

So Austin remembered her teeny tiny obsession with sports cars. Meanwhile he'd always talked about getting a reliable sedan—a Honda or Toyota. Something that would keep its value years after being paid off. And absolutely no red paint jobs since red cars had a higher accident rate.

"Well, people change, Austin. You of all people should know that."

The words were harsh. Her tone was harsh. But the alternative was to smile at his teasing and make the mistake of letting Austin into her life again. And she could not do that.

She refused to let this guy break her heart again.

And the worst part was Austin should have known better. He'd seen the way Milo's disappearance had shattered Harper. She was still bruised from her brother leaving when Austin had done the exact same thing.

Austin sighed. "Harper…I…"

She shook her head. "I can't do this right now. I can't make small talk about our cars because I need to focus on the task at hand. I need to keep my mind sharp while we try to find Audrey."

Harper saw him nod in her peripheral vision, and she eased her foot from the gas pedal. This was good. If they could agree to boundaries, then maybe she could survive the next few days of filming *Wedding Games*.

First, she just had to survive the next few hours with Austin while they looked for her sister.

Harper drove through Wellspring, watching the sidewalks as they drove past the general store and the coffee shop. She ignored the line of cars trailing her and how the one directly behind her rode her bumper. They could honk all they wanted—she had a job to do.

A job that would be a million times easier without Austin's constant fidgeting driving her batty.

Harper could practically feel it under her skin the way his eyes went from the rearview mirror to the side view mirror. And if he tapped on that clipboard any faster, his fingers were going to go blurry from the speed. And that cologne. It filled the car with its intoxicating smell, and Harper couldn't escape it.

"That's it," she said, suddenly jerking the wheel and pulling into a small, public parking lot. "We're walking."

Austin's answering sigh threatened to push Harper over the edge, but she quickly got out of the car and took a deep, calming breath.

There, she thought. *Much better.*

She just needed to escape the proximity to Austin. In the open air, she could breathe. She inhaled the scent of earth and exhaust. Not as appealing as freshly baked biscuits, but better than Austin's cologne reminding her of every single stupid word she'd said to him on graduation day.

She frowned. Why in the world was he still wearing the same cologne she'd given him? She shook her head. Boys were idiots about things like that. He probably didn't even realize it was the same one.

"Is everything okay?" Austin asked as he walked over to the driver's side of the car.

She rolled her eyes. *Is everything okay?* Had their years apart reduced his conversational skills to that one catchphrase?

"Uh-huh." Harper took another deep breath. "Just thought it might be easier to look for Audrey if we were walking down the sidewalk."

"Instead of slowing down traffic from here to Asheville?"

Harper glared at him. "You didn't have to come, you know. I do fine on my own."

Austin leaned against the car and scrubbed his hands through his hair. "So do you want to split up and each take a direction?"

Her heart soared at the thought of getting away but then it crashed right back down. He wanted to get away from her too.

"Do you know where you're going?" She gestured at the street they'd just turned off. "You've never been here before."

Not even once during college had he come for a visit during a break. He'd always been skiing or soaking up the sun with his sorority girl du jour. Then he'd come back after break complaining to Harper about how boring it had been.

"You did always tell me how beautiful it is here." He walked to the sidewalk and looked up and down the street. "But in the interest of not getting lost and losing even more time, I think we should stick together."

Harper narrowed her eyes. "You never get lost."

He threw his hands in the air. "And we're wasting time arguing. Can we just go, please?"

Without a word, Harper huffed off toward the sidewalk. The two walked in silence down the street toward the Flour Girl Bakery. Harper slowed down at every store to peer inside. And, at every store, the people working behind the counters all waved at her. She struggled to keep her face relaxed and carefree as she gave an answering wave. And with each store, it became easier.

This was her home. These were her people. And just knowing that she was surrounded by familiar faces made it easier for her to spend this much time with Austin. When he left at the end of filming—which he inevitably would—it was comforting to know that Harper wouldn't be alone.

Not like last time.

Harper continued to smile and wave and covertly look for Audrey as they walked down the sidewalk toward Flour Girl. But with each store they passed, Harper's heart sunk a little bit more. She didn't see Audrey anywhere, and they were less than a block from her bakery.

The smell of baked bread hit her nostrils before they turned the corner. But even that reassuring scent wasn't enough to lift her spirits.

Audrey really was gone.

EIGHT

5 Days Until Dream Wedding

AUSTIN FELT like a kid on Christmas. He'd heard everyone on set talk about Flour Girl Bakery, and he'd tasted the treats Harper had provided for the production crew, but he'd been setting up lighting in the dining room the night some of the crew had gone down to Harper's bakery for filming.

And without the excuse of visiting for work, it hadn't felt right for Austin to go to Flour Girl. It felt too much like spying. And maybe it was. He'd spent the last four years wondering how Harper was doing. She'd completely thrown him off with her surprise announcement at graduation, even if it had been exactly what he wanted. But he had a plan for how things would go: they'd go to California together, he'd get a job, and then he could make his move. He wanted to be everything for her, and there she was, telling him she wanted him then, no money, no plan, no proof he could be who she needed him to be.

Who wouldn't freak out at that?

So he'd left. Just walked away in search of a quiet

place to think. By the time he'd worked out a new plan, she'd already left to head back to Wellspring. He knew how temperamental she could be and figured he'd get the typical "sorry for being a drama queen" text soon enough and have his chance to explain. But then the days passed with no messages from her, he knew his window for forgiveness had closed—possibly forever.

Sure, he could have reached out on social media. She hadn't blocked him, just unfriended and kept her profile private. He'd been staring at the same profile picture for months, wondering who'd taken it and where she was. Of course, they still had friends in common that he could have asked, but Austin didn't have the right to do that. And even if he had, what would he have said?

Maybe "is everything okay?"

His face burned as he realized how many times he'd asked her that in one day.

Austin wasn't usually this careless with his words or his actions. But being around Harper did something to him. It mixed up his brain, it made him lose track of the many things that he'd considered vital only a week ago.

He dragged his mind back to the present—and the very real emergency they were dealing with—and followed Harper into the bakery. Once inside, he closed his eyes and breathed in the smell of bread. The aroma made him weirdly nostalgic even though it wasn't the first time he'd been around baked goods since college.

When he opened his eyes and looked around the small bakery, his breath caught in his chest. Even though he'd seen some of the footage of Flour Girl Bakery, seeing it in person was an entirely different experience.

Austin could see Harper's hand in everything. From

the eclectic decor of bright, mismatched tables and chairs scattered around the space, to the handwritten chalkboard menu and the artwork on the walls. Everything screamed unpredictable and unique Harper. And yet, there was order to everything. A sense of order that had been missing the last time he'd seen Harper.

Each piece of seemingly haphazard furniture had a place, making it easy to navigate and move around the small space. And when Austin's gaze went to the counter, the pastries were all aligned in beautiful rows—even though they all had weird flavors and names.

Seeing Harper's bakery gave Austin the smallest glimpse into what she'd been up to all these years, and he was so proud of her. She'd somehow managed to get organized and serious without losing herself in the process.

What an amazing feat.

"Hey, Tiffany. How's the birthday party order coming along?" Harper asked, bringing Austin back into the present.

The teenager in an "all you knead is love" shirt behind the counter smiled. "I finished it this morning. It's all packed up and ready to go."

Harper nodded. "Perfect. And the wedding cake for Saturday?"

Tiffany's smile grew. "The cakes should be finished cooling and are ready for their crumb coat. Everything's out, and I was planning on getting to that as soon as I finished straightening up the display case."

"Hmm." Harper looked down at her watch and up at Austin. "What time is Sienna and Fox's interview supposed to be?"

He looked down at his clipboard because, yes, he

was still carrying that stupid thing around. Even as he tried to enjoy Harper's bakery, *Wedding Games* and the need for everything to run smoothly hummed in the back of his mind. "Not until three. Why?"

"I'm taking a break to frost a cake."

Austin's mouth fell open. "Frost a *cake*? An entire wedding cake?"

She narrowed her eyes at him, but he glared right back. There was too much going on to stop and play baker. For all her growing up, it looked like Harper was just as unpredictable as always.

"How long will that take?" He clicked his pen and held it over his clipboard, ready to dive into problem solving mode.

"It's just the crumb coat. Less than an hour with making the buttercream."

Austin looked at the front door, his watch, and back to Harper. "Are you sure that's a great idea? We've already been gone close to an hour. And if Au—" He glanced at Tiffany wiping down a table on the other side of the room and cleared his throat. "If the thing we need isn't in town, we'll need a new plan to find it."

"I know, but I've been trying to balance work and the show and..." She took a deep breath. "Baking is one of the things that can calm me down no matter what. And I'm afraid if I don't go back there right now, Audrey might not be the only one who goes missing."

Austin's eyes went wide and went to Tiffany, who was still across the room but it was a very small room. Did Harper want everyone to know the dilemma they were in? Though her employee probably didn't know Bruce, or even a way to get in contact with the producer, every single person who knew what was going on was an extra liability. A liability they didn't need right now.

"Shh. You shouldn't say that so loud." He jerked his head toward Harper's employee. *Well that's a phrase I never thought I'd say. "Harper's employee."*

Harper rolled her eyes, and without turning her head toward the pony-tailed girl behind her, called over her shoulder. "Hey, Tiffany."

"Yes?"

"Are you going to sell Audrey and me to the network for a monetary reward?"

Tiffany laughed. "Depends. How much are you talking?"

Harper shrugged, her eyes still trained on Austin.

His brows lowered as he tried to figure out what she was getting at.

"I don't know. A thousand. Ten thousand. Does it matter?" Harper asked.

"Nope. I think I'd rather work here than get some snitch check."

Harper laughed again. "Good, because I doubt they'd give you anything."

Tiffany shrugged. "Then I guess I made the right choice."

Harper gave Austin a triumphant grin before she turned and faced Tiffany. "Austin and I are going in the back to frost that cake. If anyone comes looking for us, we aren't here." She paused. "Unless it's Audrey. Then you lock her in and tell us."

Tiffany gave her a small salute. "Sure thing."

Harper thanked her, and Austin was helpless to do anything but follow her as she walked into the kitchen. It was smaller than the one at Emerald Inn, and even though Austin didn't know anything about mixers, it was obvious Harper's equipment was not as fancy as Marcey's.

But it was hers, and she was in full command here as she unwrapped sticks of butter and put them in the mixing bowl.

And even though he should have been freaking out about the detour and concerned about finding Audrey, Austin was impressed for the second time since walking through the door of Harper's bakery. "This is really amazing."

Harper stopped peeling the plastic and looked up at Austin. "What? Butter?"

"No, this." He waved his hand around the kitchen. "You've always been so good at baking, and you turned that passion into a career. It's amazing."

Harper mumbled something as she went back to putting butter in the mixing bowl.

He shook his head and chuckled. She'd always been horrible at taking a compliment. How many times had he told her that her baking was the best thing he'd ever had, only to have her fire back with all the things she wished she'd done differently?

Well, it wasn't happening today. Austin was determined to make Harper see herself as the amazing woman that she was. It might not make a difference now in how she felt about him, but he had to try.

He pulled a stool over to the counter where she was busy measuring powdered sugar. "Seriously, Harper. Look at this place. You've followed your dreams and made Flour Girl a reality. How many people can say that?"

She turned the mixer on and, without meeting

Austin eyes, she said, "Yeah, well...my mom helped me with a small loan to get this place started. Without that, I would have never been able to do this on my own."

Austin sighed. "Maybe so. But you took that money and made it work for you. It's obvious your employees love you. And you're making a wedding cake."

She shook her head. "I make wedding cakes all the time."

Austin leaned forward and put his hands on the steel countertop. "Exactly. People trust you to make their cake on their special day."

A small smile tugged at her lips. "Well, when you put it that way."

"I do." He leaned back and watched Harper as she added the sugar, vanilla, and a splash of cream to the butter inside the mixing bowl. She carefully watched it as the machine blended ingredients together into a batch of smooth, white frosting.

Harper stopped the mixer and grabbed a spoon from one of the drawers. She dipped it into the frosting and put it to her lips. Austin couldn't pull his eyes away as her lips closed around the spoon. How had he watched her bake treat after treat in college and not realized how undeniably attractive she was when she was baking. Or taste-testing.

He cleared his throat.

Harper looked up and blushed. "Oh, I wasn't thinking. Do you want to try it?"

No, what he wanted to do was pull Harper into his arms and kiss her like crazy. But instead, he nodded. "Sure."

She opened the drawer and grabbed a clean spoon. After loading it with a dollop of frosting, she handed it over to Austin. When he reached out and took it from her, the brush of her fingers against his sent waves of electricity up his arm.

"It's delicious," he said, after putting the spoon to his lips. It had the perfect blend of sugar and vanilla, without that weird chemical taste that came from frosting in a can.

She bit her bottom lip. "Thanks."

"You're welcome."

The two looked at each other a moment longer, Austin's heart thumping away, begging him to do or say something. Anything. The second he opened his mouth, Harper started moving again. She pulled a cake from the refrigerator and set it on a rotating cake stand. Then she grabbed a plastic, triangle bag and filled it with frosting.

"So, tell me about what you're doing," Austin said, the silence too heavy.

Harper walked him through the crumb coat as she spread a thin layer of frosting on the cake. She explained that it was something bakers did to make the actual frosting easier and that the cakes would go back in the refrigerator when she was done.

"Wait, so how long does it take to make a cake?"

"It depends." She shrugged as she turned the cake stand and made sure the entire thing was covered. "It can take a few days from start to finish depending on how difficult it is."

"Wow," Austin breathed. "The skill and patience involved is really impressive."

Harper dipped her chin, hiding her face. But not before Austin caught a glimpse of the smug smile on her lips.

They didn't say anything else while Harper finished up the crumb coat and put the cakes back into the refrigerator. He let himself relax into the familiarity of watching her do what she loved and allowed the smell of sugar and cinnamon to waft over him. But when she started putting the dirty dishes in the large sink, Austin got up from his spot on the stool and walked over.

In college, the arrangement had always been that Harper would make something amazing for them to eat, and Austin was on cleanup duty. He started running the water, and once it was hot enough, he put the stopper in and added some soap.

"Austin, you don't—"

"I know. But I want to."

Harper nodded. "Okay, but I have a few more regulations I have to follow these days."

She walked him through the proper way to wash, rinse and sanitize the dishes. In no time they were finished, and just like Harper had promised, it had taken less than an hour, including cleanup.

When the last dish was stacked in a much neater cabinet than Austin had ever seen in Harper's dorm room, she looked up at him with a small smile. "Thank you."

"I don't mind getting my hands pruny."

"No." She looked down at her feet. "I mean for not huffing and puffing while I frosted the cake. I know it took forever, but I feel much better having worked on something here."

"Good." So did Austin, surprisingly. The satisfying swish of the whirling mixer blades, and the slow and careful way Harper smoothed frosting onto the cakes had been hypnotizing and calming.

It was the perfect moment to tell her how he felt. Well, technically, the perfect moment would have been a half second after she told him she loved him four years ago. She'd moved on, but she deserved to know.

Right now, just do it.

Harper looked back up at him. "But I think it's time for us to get back to looking for Audrey."

"I think that sounds like a good idea. Where to next?"

"Let's go check out Audrey's apartment."

NINE

5 Days Until Dream Wedding

THE CALM that came with being in Flour Girl's kitchen disappeared precisely two point three seconds after Harper and Austin got into her car again. If Austin washing the dishes wasn't enough to muddle Harper's thinking, the fact that his stupid cologne permeated the air in her car—again—made her crazy.

Thankfully, it was only a ten-minute drive to Audrey's apartment, and Harper turned the radio on to keep Austin from giving her any more compliments about her bakery. It was sweet of him to be so impressed. Too sweet, really. She just couldn't listen to that right now. She needed her head clear and her emotions under control.

When Harper pulled up to her sister's apartment, Audrey's parking space was empty. Harper blinked back tears and turned off the car. She really thought her sister would be here. There was nowhere else she could be, and time was running out. If she and Austin didn't get back to The Emerald Inn soon, then they'd both be in trouble, and Bruce would find out.

"Any updates from the inn?" Harper asked, stalling while she considered her options. Go inside and confirm that Audrey was really gone, or head back now and admit defeat?

"Nope." His walkie-talkie had been silent since they left, and Harper's phone hadn't buzzed once.

"Do you think we should call Sienna to see what's up?"

Austin shook his head. "It's too risky. If someone overhears, we're all cooked."

"Or baked?"

He groaned, then unbuckled his seatbelt. "Should we take a look?"

Austin followed Harper up the stairs to the second story of the building. After she'd fished out her keys and unlocked the front door, he held the door for her to walk inside.

The bright white and blue apartment was quiet, and the living room was still. The kind of still that no one had disturbed in at least a week.

"Doesn't look like she's here," Austin said.

Harper spun around. "You think?"

He lifted his hands and took a step back. "I'm just wondering if we should try somewhere else. Eli's apartment maybe? See if she's snuggling with Mister Mittens in yours?"

Harper shook her head, and her eyes continued to search the small apartment. "Tiffany's feeding my cat during filming and would have mentioned if she'd seen anything unusual at my apartment."

Austin raised his eyebrows. "You trust her a lot for someone so young."

"She's reliable. I've gotten better at recognizing who I can count on."

Austin's cheeks flushed pink, but he didn't say anything. Harper took a deep breath and reminded herself Austin was going out on a limb to help her.

"Maybe she left some kind of clue," she said, and began to hunt around for a receipt for a hotel, a plane ticket, anything that might tell Harper where her sister had gone.

But there was nothing. Every surface was clean and clutter free.

She knew there wouldn't be any traces. This wasn't the 90s. People didn't keep paper receipts for anything. If Audrey had booked a hotel or a flight, she'd have the confirmation on her phone.

Harper suppressed the frustrated growl. Where was Audrey?

"So this is where Audrey lives," Austin said. He trailed behind her as she rifled through drawers and flipped through books. There was a pristine copy of *The Joy Of Baking* sitting on a shelf that Harper didn't even bother to open.

"Yep. She's had it for the last few years. It's going to be weird when she doesn't live here anymore." The hours Harper had spent here, laughing and baking with her sister had been some of the happiest memories in recent years. It made her forget all the pain that someone standing very close to her right now had caused her. And the even older pain both Audrey and Harper carried around from Milo's absence.

Austin walked around the small living room, hands in his pockets. "It's just cool to finally get a glimpse of your family. One that doesn't involve *Wedding Games*."

"Don't these shows do like, a ton of research on people before they sign them up? To make sure there are no ax murderers or Justin Bieber fans or anything?"

"The studio does have a strict no-Belieber policy." Austin's lips pulled up into a half-smile. "I was brought in last minute when someone dropped out. Jennifer did most of the research."

Harper frowned. She'd seen the name Jennifer on a badge hanging around the neck of a skinny, pretty brunette who always seemed to be hovering around Austin.

"You've worked with her before?"

"On a few projects," Austin said. "She was one of the first people I met out in LA. She's great."

They were in the minuscule kitchen now, and he opened up each cabinet to look inside carefully.

"I know my sister is tiny compared to me, but I don't think she'd fit inside there."

"Like you said, maybe there's a clue here." He gestured at a half-empty cabinet. "Look, all her plates and cookware are gone. Does that mean she's moved in somewhere else?"

Harper shook her head and laughed. "If you knew her at all, the state of her cabinets wouldn't seem suspicious. She's a terrible cook and eats out or at Eli's at least five times a week."

Austin closed the cabinet and looked Harper in the eye. "I would have liked to have met your family before."

Harper inhaled sharply and bit back a catty reply. Austin probably knew Jennifer's family pretty well by now, he didn't need to know Harper's.

At first she'd been relieved she'd never mentioned

him to her family while she'd been at college. He was just one of her friends, grouped together with others when she'd told her stories. She'd never given a hint to anyone what she'd felt for him, thank goodness. It meant there was no one to pity her when it had all blown up in her face. No one to tell her "I told you so" that a guy like him could never love a girl like her.

But now, she regretted the secrecy. It was the reason no one could understand why she was so out of it those first few days of filming. Seeing Austin had been a kick in the gut, and there was no one she'd been able to talk to about it.

"Well," she said. "Now you've met everyone. Including my future brother-in-law."

"They all seem great," he said and leaned against the kitchen island. "Well, except that Harry guy. He seems kind of rude and doesn't talk to Reagan that nicely."

Harper's heart swelled. Audrey and Harper had been debating for months if they should tell Reagan what a jerk they thought Harry was. To hear Austin reach that same conclusion in a matter of days was intensely gratifying.

"She's like the fourth Hudson sister." Harper sat down on a stool across from Austin. "She really stepped in to support Audrey when Milo left. She was in her freshman year at college. Eli didn't know what to do when that happened. Without Reagan there, she probably would have dropped out. Then this whole reality show wedding may never have happened."

"You never told me that." Austin reached out a hand toward Harper, then seemed to reconsider and drew it back. She bit her lip. Was she disappointed or relieved?

"You know I don't like to talk about him," she said, and turned her head to look out the window above the sink. The view of the parking lot was not so interesting, but she knew the bedroom had a great view of the mountains. She should probably look there, too, but was rooted to the stool. Any mention or thought of Milo still took her a minute to work through, even though over ten years had passed.

"I know you think you'll never see him again, but you never know," Austin said, and Harper whipped her head around to glare at him. He paled under her intense gaze. "I mean, I never thought I'd see you again and look what happened. All it took was a bit of randomness and a production assistant with mono and here we both are on the set of *Wedding Games*."

Harper squeezed her eyes shut and pressed her palms into them while a storm of feelings collided inside of her. Austin probably thought she was trying not to cry, and maybe she was. The hope of seeing her brother again that she usually shoved as far down as possible surged to the surface. Maybe it really was as simple as a random chance. Maybe that's all that had pulled him away in the first place. She'd been in high school, old enough to know something was going on with him, but what twenty-two year old would confide in his sixteen-year old sister? It must have been something beyond his control, to keep him away for so long.

Yet she was much less forgiving to Austin. He'd had his chance with her, and he blew it. Her fury at the universe for pushing Austin into her path was second only to her anger at herself for how giddy she got every time his deep amber eyes focused on her. She peeked through her hands to see him doing that right now and cursed her heart for being a big vat of Jell-O instead of the rock-hard, dried out chunk of brown sugar she needed it to be.

Then, like the sudden sizzle of butter in a hot pan, worry spread itself through her chest. She dropped her hands to her sides and stood up. Had she forgotten to close the refrigerator door properly at the bakery?

"We should probably get back," she said. She couldn't do anything about her feelings about Milo or Austin, but she could at least make sure the wedding cake wasn't ruined. "Can we stop by the bakery on the way? I just need to check something." She could call Tiffany but didn't want Austin to hear Harper admit to possibly having made a mistake.

Austin nodded, turned away from the counter, then stopped in his tracks.

"What's that?" He pointed toward the refrigerator.

"A refrigerator. Don't you have those in LA?"

He clicked his tongue. "That photo of the four of you. Where are you?"

Harper walked around the island and pushed past Austin to get a closer look. Her arm tingled where her skin had brushed against his T-shirt.

You can't count on him, don't even think about it.

The photo was held up with a Clingmans Dome magnet, halfway hidden behind a grocery list and a The Brew House coupon. She shouldn't have been surprised that he'd been able to spot it. His eye for detail had been downright annoying back in college, but today, it might actually be useful.

"That's Eli's parents' cabin. We went right before I graduated high school, just the girls. Gosh, I'd forgotten about that trip. Sienna looks so young."

"You all look happy," said Austin as he pulled away the magnet and held the picture carefully. "Where is it?"

Harper had to think about it. "It's about an hour and a half from here. We only went that one time all four girls, it was more a place for Eli and Audrey to escape to."

She gasped as the words left her mouth and turned to Austin.

"Do you think...?"

His eyes were wide with excitement. "We have to at least take a look, right?"

Harper nodded, not trusting herself to speak.

"I'll drive," he said, and held out his hand for the keys.

"Absolutely not."

TEN

5 Days Until Dream Wedding

AUSTIN GRIPPED the door handle and tried to breathe normally. "Do we need to be driving so fast?"

Harper looked over at him, her eyebrows sky high. "I'm barely ten above the limit."

"Just watch the road!"

"Austin, please, I could drive these roads blindfolded."

He wouldn't mind a blindfold right about now. The roads here were so different from the ones in LA. The giant highways were always packed to the gills. Traffic always crawled and even the shortest commutes took forever.

Here, the two-lane highways that snaked through the mountains were almost deserted. It was rare that they saw another car coming from the other direction. But every time Austin saw headlights appear from around the curve of the roads, he struggled to catch his breath.

Add to that a speed limit that was far too high considering that short guardrails were the only barrier between them and falling down the side of the mountains, and this drive was one of the most stressful experiences of Austin's life.

He'd always hated letting others drive, not trusting that they wouldn't get distracted. Without the focus needed to drive, his mind went to all of the dangerous possibilities for a car speeding down a highway. But one look at Harper's face at the empty apartment, and he knew there was no way she was relinquishing control of her car.

Before they left, Austin called Bruce to let him know he needed to drop something off at the bridal salon for tomorrow's filming. Bruce hadn't even asked where he'd been this whole time, which should have been a relief, but only put Austin on edge. The demanding producer never missed an opportunity to yell at someone. Whatever Sienna and Fox were doing must be keeping everyone very busy. Meanwhile, Harper called Tiffany to tell her that if anyone from the production called, to make up a huge baking emergency that Harper was too busy dealing with to come to the phone.

But, so far, no one had called. Harper seemed to have realized this at the same moment as Austin. The car slowed down the tiniest bit, and she turned to him. "Do you think Sienna and Fox have it under control?"

"We've been gone for hours. The only reason no one has noticed we're not there is if there's something super interesting happening." He crossed his fingers that it was true, and that they'd get to the cabin in one piece.

"And it'll be another two, at least, before we're back." The car started to pick up speed again.

"I thought you said this place was an hour and a half away?"

She didn't say anything, but the car barreled even faster down the narrow road.

"Harper, please." He closed his eyes, unable to look at the trees as they rushed by in a blur. He regretted not grabbing the Dramamine he'd packed before flying out to Wellspring. He hadn't needed it all week, but then again, he hadn't been passenger to Harper driving Grand Prix style through the Blue Ridge Parkway either. His stomach churned. "I think I may be sick."

"Not in here. I make deliveries in this car."

She let up on the accelerator and drove at the legal speed for more than a few seconds. Austin relaxed his grip on the door handle and opened his eyes.

Harper was staring straight ahead, her hands clenching the steering wheel so tightly her knuckles were white.

"Hey." He reached out and touched her arm. "I'm sure she'll be there. She probably just needed to get away for the day to relax."

Harper shook her head, and a tear fell from her eye. "She would have told me. This is so unlike her, just to bail and not say anything. That's not what the Hudson women do." She wiped a hand under her nose and sniffed. "It's what the men do."

And what Austin had done. The crush of guilt that he'd been pushing away all day suddenly settled in his shoulders like a production camera was strapped on him. He wanted to say the words. He needed her to hear them. But as the miles flew by, he kept his mouth shut.

What could he say, really? *I'm sorry* just didn't seem like enough. *I've always loved you and still do* was just way over the top. She'd laugh in his face and tell him it was too late.

He had to accept that there was no plan he could devise that would make things better with Harper. The best he could do was to help her find her sister and save *Wedding Games* from total disaster. He would tuck away the new memories of her from this crazy adventure, and she'd go back to being just another cast member the second they got back to the inn with Audrey.

"You're being awfully quiet." Harper glanced at him. "That used to mean you were thinking big thoughts."

"More like too many thoughts." He rubbed his hands over his face. He'd been counting on a boring day doing cast interviews. All the running around combined with resisting the urge every other second to pull Harper into his arms was starting to wear on him. "Would you be super mad if I shut my eyes for a power nap?"

The corners of her mouth ticked up. "I forgot you used to take those in between classes. It was like your superpower. You could fall asleep in seconds then wake up fifteen minutes later like you'd slept all night."

He grinned. "It's definitely comes in handy in my line of work."

"Fetching coffee for big shots like Bruce?"

"More like saving the world."

She laughed, and the sound was like a direct current straight to his heart. "Wow, barely four years in California and you've already got the big LA ego."

"Hey, you were the one who called it a superpower."

He smiled at her, and after a second's hesitation, she smiled back. Suddenly, he wasn't so tired anymore.

Austin sat up in his seat and tried to focus on the road to keep his queasy stomach from getting worse.

"I thought you were going to take a power nap."

Austin chuckled. "Yeah, well turns out I'm going to take in this gorgeous scenery instead."

And it was gorgeous. The random tiny waterfalls on the side of the mountains, strange orange flowers that seemed to pop up randomly throughout the forest, the rare breaks in the tree lines that gave Austin a view of the surrounding area.

It was nothing like California. And while the state he'd called home since college was beautiful in its own way, it couldn't compare to the lush green of the Blue Ridge Mountains. Or the natural beauty of Harper's smile.

"I love driving through this area. The ebb and flow of the road makes it easy to process certain things. Sometimes I take a drive when I'm struggling with something. It's the worst for deliveries though."

The small glimpse of vulnerability shocked Austin. It was like seeing the old Harper again. Austin wondered if he'd see more of this side of her the longer he spent with her. Austin secretly hoped that Audrey wasn't at the cabin when they got there so he could find out, then felt like a horrible person. Harper was worried sick, and all he could think about was eking out a few more hours with her.

He stared out the window as he processed Harper's words about the twisty roads. And if it wasn't for the motion sickness Austin was battling, he would agree with her. Now that Harper was driving the speed limit, he could appreciate the hypnotic back and forth of the car as they went up the mountain and then down—even if he wanted to barf.

"Do you think anyone is going to be waiting for us at the cabin?" Austin asked.

"I'm hoping Audrey is."

Austin shook his head. "I mean, besides her. I know Eli and his parents are back at The Emerald Inn, but are there any aunts, uncles, or cousins that I should be aware of?"

"Wouldn't you like to know."

Austin let out a short breath through his nose and tried to stay calm. Whatever vulnerability she'd hinted at was closed off tight again. "Yes. Yes, I would."

Harper laughed and looked away from the road long enough to send a saucy wink his way.

She was messing with him. Flirting maybe? The idea of Harper letting down her guard enough to playfully wink at him made his heart soar. He wasn't expecting things to go back to the way they were—that was impossible. But maybe they could rebuild their friendship.

The idea was both exciting and disappointing. He missed Harper, but he didn't want friendship. He wanted more. He wanted to go back to that day when she'd so boldly confessed her feelings and pull her into his arms and kiss her senseless.

He wanted to go back and knock some sense into twenty-two-year-old Austin and tell him not to be an idiot.

"The answer is no, by the way," Harper said after a few minutes of silence. "The only people who have keys are Eli and his family."

Austin's stomach fell. He hadn't even considered that they'd need keys to get in. It felt like such a rookie mistake. He was making every mistake. "How are we going to get in?"

"Relax. I swiped Audrey's spare key from her junk drawer before we left." She pointed to her purse that was on the floor of the passenger seat. "You didn't think I'd suggest we drive all the way of to the cabin without a way to get in, did you?"

Austin hadn't thought of it. He was not on top of things like he should be. Harper was thinking of every detail while he bumbled around and tried not to get sick in her car. Everything was all mixed up.

When Austin didn't respond, Harper started laughing. "Oh my goodness. You didn't even think about the keys."

"I was a little distracted," Austin mumbled.

It only made Harper laugh harder. "Oh, I like this version of Austin who isn't perfect and forgets things. It makes the rest of us look better."

"You've always been my better half."

The words were out before Austin could think twice about it, and Harper instantly sobered. Her posture was rigid as she stared out the front windshield. Both hands gripped the steering wheel, and the silence between them was heavy.

Austin so badly wanted to know what was going on inside her head, but he didn't dare speak, so he turned on the radio without asking. When she didn't comment on his choice of music, he knew she was completely lost in her own thoughts. The next thirty minutes dragged on. Each time the clock on her dash ticked over another minute, Austin felt like it had been about eight hundred seconds.

Eventually, Harper spoke. "The cabin is just a couple minutes away."

Austin sat up straight in his seat. Good. Her attention needed to be on Audrey, not Austin's dozens of mistakes today. He looked out the window as Harper turned off the highway and onto a small side road. A few short moments later, they were bouncing onto a dirt road. It led them deeper into the woods, and Austin bit his lip to keep from asking if it was the right way. Finally, Austin spotted a mailbox and a steep gravel driveway and let out a sigh of relief.

It was so steep that Austin wondered if Harper's older vehicle would be able to make it up safely. But she didn't hesitate and turned toward it. "Uh, Harper?"

She pressed down on the accelerator, and gravel from the driveway flung out under her tires. "Yeah?" she said through gritted teeth, not taking her eyes from the driveway.

"Are you sure your car..." Austin cleared his throat, unsure how to express his concern without starting another argument about who knew Wellspring and its surrounding areas better.

"My car is awesome."

With one final push, and a satisfied smirk from Harper, the car jerked forward and they were at the top of the incline. The car shuddered to a stop in front of the cabin. It was no match for the luxury of The Emerald Inn, but it was bigger than he expected.

"We're here," Harper announced with a tremble in her voice.

Austin followed her out of the car and looked around. Harper's car was the only vehicle here, and his heart sank. Their search would, once again, come up empty.

He wasn't sure if Harper had already come to the same conclusion, but she fished the keys out of her purse and unlocked the front door in record time. She didn't say a word as she went through every room, opening every door and cabinet.

Austin trailed behind her, each silent step heavier than the last. Just like Audrey's apartment, the cabin was empty. All the lights were off, and there was a slightly stale scent in the air. No one had been to the cabin in weeks, maybe months.

Harper threw her purse on the ground with a curse. "I really thought she'd be here."

He opened his mouth to say something reassuring. Something like they could keep looking, or that they'd find Audrey. But nothing felt like enough. He wasn't enough.

Harper turned to Austin, her shoulders sagging. "Come on. Let's go back. We'll just explain to Bruce what happened and hope that it's not as bad as we think it's going to be."

Austin was pretty sure it was going to be just as bad, or worse. He'd be fired, the show would be ruined, and who knew what horrible things Bruce could do with the footage they'd already gotten. The last thing Austin wanted to do was go back to the inn, but he followed her out to her car anyway. He had the hour-and-a-half drive back to The Emerald Inn to come up with a new plan to save the show—and his last chance at Harper's heart.

ELEVEN

5 Days Until Dream Wedding

HARPER SLAMMED her hands against the steering wheel for the third time. This could not be happening. She'd bought this station wagon instead of her dream car because it was supposed to be practical. It had trunk space for deliveries, four-wheel drive for the mountains, and a reliable engine.

Or at least, she thought it was reliable.

Less than a mile from Eli's cabin and the stupid thing started making a loud noise. At first, Harper just ignored it. Ninety-five percent of her problems usually worked themselves out if she left them alone long enough. But then the noise got louder, and Austin's fidgeting more frantic, Harper pulled over to the side of the dirt road that led to the cabin and turned the car off.

"When was the last time you got a tune up?"

"Uh, the last time I had a day off, which would be never. I have a business to run."

Austin frowned. "Regular maintenance saves money in the long term."

Harper's jaw clenched tight. Starting a fight right now wouldn't be helpful.

But it sure would make her feel better.

"If you know so much about cars, go out and fix it."

Without a word, Austin opened the door and stalked to the front of the car. He waved a hand at her and she popped the hood.

Harper fought the urge to roll her eyes. Of course he knew about cars. He knew how to fix everything. His brain was like a dictionary of random facts. In college, whenever he started dating a new girl, he'd absorb all her interests and hobbies. The super focus and planning he put to use in his classes worked even better for being the perfect boyfriend. The girls loved it, loved him, and had no idea he spent his Thursday nights with Harper watching *Battlestar Galactica*, his *real* favorite show.

Austin's head disappeared behind the hood, and Harper wondered what his favorite was now. She wondered what random movies and shows he'd had to learn about to make Jennifer follow him around the way she did.

Harper sat with her arms crossed, stewing in bad memories and hurt feelings. Austin remained hidden, doing mysterious things to the car. Five minutes passed, then ten. He went to the trunk to pull out the toolbox Eli had made her stash there, along with blankets and a candle to melt snow in case she got stranded somewhere alone.

Now she actually was stranded, but she wasn't alone.

She got out of the car and stomped over to Austin, intent on making him as miserable as she was.

"How's it going, Fonzie?"

He glanced up at her, the wrench in his hand on

something big and important looking.

"Fonzie? That's your go-to mechanic reference?"

She shrugged. "I forgot you don't like *Happy Days*." She hadn't forgotten, she'd wanted to irk him.

But he wasn't irked, he was intense. He moved around the engine like he'd done it a thousand times, pulling things out to check and make adjustments.

It would be easier to hate him if he weren't so freaking hot.

But she didn't hate him. Yes, he'd hurt her, but she'd never stopped loving him, not really. How could she? Look where he was. He was in the middle of the woods when he should be at his job. A job he'd wanted so badly, he'd defied his parents and chosen film school over medical school. A job she had apparently pushed him toward even more when she'd blurted out all the feelings in her heart four years ago.

Austin stood up and wiped his hands on the rag he'd slung over his shoulder at some point. "You wanna give it a try?"

Harper's head whipped up. "What, us?"

The corner of his mouth twitched. "The car."

Duh. Harper hid her rapidly heating cheeks behind her hair and practically ran to the door and threw herself in. She took a deep breath before turning the key. It would work, they'd go back to the inn, Audrey would be there, and she'd never have to talk to Austin again.

The engine turned once, then died.

Austin actually jumped back at the scream that ripped out of Harper's throat.

"Are you okay?" He yanked the door open and put his arms on her shoulders. "Did I mess something up?"

"Yes. No." Tears sprang to the corners of her eyes. "I just want this to be over."

He kept his hands on her shoulders and squeezed. "So we'll go back to the inn. I'll get a rideshare." The tightness in her chest loosened a bit at the calm smile on his face. Austin would fix this. He could fix anything.

Just not her broken heart, unfortunately.

Austin's smile quickly disappeared when he looked down at his phone. "Uh, do you have a signal?"

With a pounding heart, she reached into her bag. She knew without even looking that there would be no bars. This far up in the mountain, she should have thought of it. It was spotty at best on a good day. But she hadn't been thinking during the drive up here. All her focus had been on Audrey. She'd been counting on Austin to take care of the details, just like always.

Except he hadn't thought of that either, and why should he? After all, she'd been insisting all day that this was *her* town, *her* mountain.

And just then, her mountain decided it was time for a summer thunderstorm.

Austin ran to the other side of the car and jumped in. "I'm sure it'll be over soon. Then we can walk down to the highway."

Harper shook her head. "This late in the day, it'll last for hours."

"Then we can't stay in the car all night. We'll freeze."

"I know it's not sunny California, but fifty degrees is still above freezing. We'll be fine."

Austin pressed his fingers to his temples. "We should head back to the cabin. Maybe there's a radio or something."

"I don't remember seeing one, do you?"

"No, but what good does it do to stay cramped here in this car? Harper, just listen to me, for once, please."

"All I've been doing all day is listen to you!" She turned to face him, her face hot. "We wasted time at the inn looking for her when I told you she wasn't there, and it was you who spotted the picture of the cabin and dragged us up here. You can't plan your way out of everything. Sometimes things just go badly, and there's nothing you can do about it."

One look at Austin's wounded expression, and she knew she'd gone too far. She was taking everything out on him, when all he'd been doing all day was trying to help her. He'd only be in her life another few days, and then she could go back to her quiet, Austin-free existence. There was no need to make the guy cry just so she could feel better for a few minutes.

As hard as it was, Harper swallowed her pride and said quietly, "But maybe we should go to the cabin until we can come up with a plan. Together."

———

AUSTIN WAS beyond thrilled that Harper agreed to his plan. He was not about to risk their safety sitting inside a cramped car, no matter how well she claimed to know these mountains. But now that they were inside the cabin, he was faced with uninterrupted alone time with Harper and wasn't sure if he was terrified or elated.

They were both soaking wet, of course, after trekking up the side of the mountain. Harper dropped her wet shoes and bag in the middle of the floor, then, without a word, she rushed into the bathroom off the kitchen. Minutes later, Austin heard the sound of water running.

Oh man. A hot shower would have been amazing, but he knew the day had been really hard for Harper and was happy to give her all the time she needed. Though, if she was still the shower hog she'd been in college, it was safe to assume she'd be a while.

He took off his wet shirt, wrung it out in the kitchen sink and draped it over the back of one of the dining room chairs. His pants were trickier. He couldn't exactly do the same as his shirt, so he used a towel to dry them off the best he could before cleaning up the small mess they'd made coming in. There were little pools of water everywhere, and Harper's shoes were not just wet, but muddy. He placed hers next to where he'd put his just inside the door as soon as he'd walked in.

He found cleaning supplies in the kitchen and got to work mopping the floor. Once he got started, it made sense to just keep going. If they'd be here all night, it might as well be clean and comfortable.

Cleaning the cabin was soothing. Nothing else today seemed to be going to plan, but at least he could control this. Looking around the shining kitchen and dust-free living room lowered his pulse at least fifty beats per minute. He'd just finished making the bed in one of the bedrooms and was fluffing the pillows when he heard the bathroom door open. Good, he'd need to clean that too.

"Austin?" Harper's voice cracked.

He rushed out, his bare feet skidding a bit on the freshly mopped floor. "I'm here. I didn't go anywhere."

Her shoulders dropped, and she smiled. Then her

eyes went wide, and with a sudden rush of heat to his face, he realized he was still shirtless.

"Let me get you a blanket," he said and turned his fiery hot face away from her. She had put her wet clothes back on. "That couldn't have been easy to go from a hot shower back into those."

"Thanks," she said when he handed her a blanket. "So what's the plan?"

His stomach clenched. Plan, yes, a plan. That was his job, not mopping floors. They'd need food and a way to contact someone, and something to do all night besides stare at each other and exchange awkward small talk.

But it was hard to think of anything other than curling up next to Harper in front of the fireplace. "Let's build a fire."

She raised an eyebrow. "With what?"

"I'm sure they keep some firewood around here somewhere."

And with that he was off again, putting the distance between them that he needed to be able to focus. He stuck his head out the back door, but all he could see were sheets of rain. Even though he'd already checked it when he had been searching for a blanket and cleaning supplies, he looked in the bedroom.

The more places he searched and came up empty, the faster his heart thumped. Maybe he could use sheets? He didn't know Eli beyond what he'd seen during filming, but Austin was sure he'd understand if they needed to burn sheets to stay warm, right?

No, he was being crazy. Austin was not going to start a fire with stuff he found in the linen closet.

When he walked back into the living room, not

entirely ready to admit that he couldn't find any wood, he pulled up short. Harper was sitting in front of the fireplace, her gray eyes fixed on the flames that were happily burning brightly.

"Where did you find firewood?"

She looked up at him, the light reflecting off her still-damp golden waves. "On the front porch."

He could have kicked himself. Of course it would be in the one place he hadn't looked.

"I guess you don't need me, do you?" He gave a weak chuckle, but his heart burned at the thought. She really didn't need him. She'd done amazing things, just like he always knew she would. And she'd done them all without him around. Without him organizing her business the way he'd done with her study schedule, or planning her days, the way he'd made sure she had enough in the fridge to eat on weekends when he went away.

"Don't say that," she said, so softly he wasn't sure he'd heard her right. But his heart nearly burst anyway. "Come sit by the fire, you're shivering."

He wanted to tell her it wasn't from the cold, but instead he grabbed another blanket from the couch and sat down on the other end of the fireplace. He was at least five feet away from her—much further than when they'd been cooped up in the car together—but he was hyper aware of every single little movement she made. She swept her wet hair off her neck and leaned a little closer to the fire.

"Careful." He reached out but pulled back when she rolled her eyes.

"I lit it myself, I think I know enough to not set my hair on fire."

"Of course you do." He pulled up his knees to wrap

the blanket around his entire body. From inside his little fort he felt a little less bare—and a little bit braver. "You can do everything now. You don't need me to plan your life like I used to."

"I didn't mind that," she said, and the quirk of her lips sent his heart racing.

He scooted back from the fire a bit, not needing its heat nearly as much as he had just a moment before.

"It made things easy for me. I didn't have to worry about anything."

"And now you worry about everything?" That was what Austin did. He'd hate to see her having to deal with the same anxiety as he did every day.

"Not always. There's just a lot on my plate right now."

Austin knew that full well. He could see the way Harper carried the guilt of Audrey leaving, even though it wasn't her fault. Had she done the same when he'd left?

Austin was afraid to know the answer, but he knew this was his chance to talk to Harper about what had happened. His heart raced, and he searched for the perfect words to finally apologize.

She stood up. "I think I'm going to try to find something dry to wear. Maybe lay down for a little bit."

Do it now, before she leaves. Before you lose your chance.

He stood up next to her and the blanket slid from his shoulders. He took a deep breath and closed his eyes. "I'm sorry."

A beat passed, then another. He cracked open an eye to peek at her reaction. She was staring into the fire, her bottom lip between her teeth. "For what?"

She wasn't going to make this easy, was she? But that

was Harper. He actually smiled a little at being able to see this glimpse of the girl he left behind. It gave him the courage to continue. "For leaving."

She inhaled sharply, and she started twisting the ends of her hair. "It's fine. I don't really think about it anymore."

"Liar."

She turned her steely gray gaze to him.

"You always play with your hair when you lie."

She dropped her hand. "I used to. You don't know me anymore. You left, remember? And then didn't bother to call or contact me for four years."

"And I have regretted it every day since then, but I just didn't know how to say it."

"You just did. You're sorry. See, all better now. Now, let me go look for those clothes."

"But it's not all better." He reached out and gently grabbed her arm. "I never stopped thinking about you, even when I wanted to. I tried so hard to get over you—"

"Get over me?" Harper shook her arm from his grip.

He took a deep breath. This was a lot harder than he thought it was going to be. "When you told me how you felt that day, it was like a thousand lightbulbs went off at once. I realized why I was never happy with the girls I dated. It was because I was in love with my best friend. I think I still am."

She took a step back. "In love with me? You sure had a funny way of showing it."

"Harper, you completely caught me off guard. I needed time to think about how to respond, but by the time I'd figured out a plan—"

Harper huffed and crossed her arms. Her glare was hotter than the flames at his back. "I wasn't asking for a plan, Austin. I was baring my soul in hopes that you felt the same way. Then you left."

He shook his head. "I know."

"That proved it for me. You didn't care about me the way I thought you did. I was humiliated and heartbroken."

"And I'm sorry."

"You already said that."

Austin put his hands out. The fire seemed unbearably hot now, and he really wished he'd found a shirt before diving into this. "I don't know what else to say. What else to do. I've spent the last four years kicking myself for thinking a plan was what I needed instead of just holding you tight and never letting go. When I saw you on the first day of filming, I thought that maybe here's my chance to make things right."

"But you ignored me. Just like you've done for the last few years."

Austin took a step toward Harper. "Would you have given me the time of day if I tried to talk to you on that first day?"

A corner of her mouth lifted. "No, probably not."

"Exactly. I wasn't sure if it would be better to leave you alone or try to explain myself. I didn't want to make another mistake, so I waited until it was obvious what I should do."

Harper lifted an eyebrow. "And?"

"And being stranded in a cabin in the middle of nowhere seems like a pretty clear sign to me."

Harper stared at Austin for a moment longer. Then, for the second time in his life, she did something that completely caught him off guard. She burst into laughter.

He blinked a few times. They'd just been arguing, and now she was laughing. Had he finally broken her?

He frowned. "It's not that funny."

"Oh, come on. It's pretty funny. We've gone four years without a single word to each other, and now we're literally forced to talk. Maybe this really is your sign." She laughed again.

He still didn't see what was so hilarious.

"And now you tell me you've been in love with me all this time, and it was just one giant misunderstanding? Okay."

His heart dropped into his stomach. She didn't believe him. Austin racked his brain as he tried to think of the words to prove to her that he was telling the truth. But words felt inadequate. He looked up at Harper. Her laughter had died down, but the smile still lingered on her face.

He knew what he needed to do. It was what he should have done when Harper first confessed her feelings at graduation. Austin took a step toward her, his heart a jackhammer in his chest. Even after walking through the rain and taking a shower, the smell of cinnamon engulfed his senses.

When he was standing just in front of her, he lifted his hand and caressed her cheek. The smile on her face fell, and her eyes went to his. They were searching for something, but Austin didn't wait to find out if she found what she was looking for. He was afraid if he waited and let his thoughts take over, he'd never do it. He *knew* he wouldn't do it.

So he leaned in and pressed his lips against hers.

Harper stiffened at the contact, and Austin instantly knew he'd gone to far. He started to pull away, endless apologies on his lips, when Harper reached out and grabbed his shoulders. Instead of pushing him away, she pulled him closer.

And kissed him back.

Austin's heart threatened to burst from his chest as his free hand wrapped around her waist and pulled her even closer. He kissed her like a starving man, and the lingering taste of vanilla on her lips was everything he needed to live.

Harper was everything he needed. This kiss was better than anything he could have dreamed up in the years they spent apart. He never wanted it to end. And for a long time, it didn't.

Eventually, the two of them pulled apart from each other. The sound of their breathing drowned out the cracking of the fire that still roared beside them. The light from the flames illuminated her skin and hair with a golden glow.

"You're so beautiful." His hand still lingered on her cheek as he took her in. He never wanted to forget this moment. With any luck, it was the first of many kisses that would be shared between them.

She stared up at him, her eyes searching just as they had before.

"I've missed you so much." He leaned down to give her another small kiss.

But Harper pulled back and shook her head. "I can't do this."

Then she ran into the bedroom and locked the door behind her.

TWELVE

5 Days Until Dream Wedding

BENEATH THE BLANKET in the only bedroom in the cabin, Harper considered her options.

She could stay here forever, mortified and alone.

Or she could go back out and explain to the one guy she'd dreamed about kissing almost every night in college why she'd run away once he'd actually kissed her.

She snuggled deeper into the bed.

Austin had made it quite nicely, considering he just had musty sheets to work with. There was somehow a fresh, clean smell to the linens, which baffled Harper. How had he managed that?

Okay, sitting here smelling the sheets was not exactly making a choice about what to do. But it helped calm her down, and she hadn't felt calm since they'd left the inn this afternoon.

Just thinking about how worried everyone must be about them sent her pulse racing again. They were in so much trouble. Everything was ruined. And instead of trying to fix it, she and Austin were making out next to the fire in the most romantic scene Harper had ever witnessed.

She closed her eyes and let herself remember the sweet words he'd just whispered. How beautiful she was, how much he had missed her. It was everything she'd ever wanted to hear from him. She sunk down into the mattress. Did it matter that it was four years late? Better late than never, right?

She groaned and covered her face with a pillow. A pillow that smelled fresh and green like the rain that was pounding on the roof.

Four years made a big difference. His life was in California. If this had happened at graduation like she'd hoped, then her life would be out there too. But it was here, in Wellspring, North Carolina—a town so tiny they combined the post office and bank. What was here for him, other than Harper? She wasn't naive enough to think she was enough to keep him here longer than a night kissing in front of the fireplace.

Sure, he'd told her he loved her. He'd also said he had loved her for the last four years, and that hadn't exactly brought him knocking down her door.

He had plans, and so did Harper. She wasn't that absent-minded girl from college anymore. She ran a successful business, for goodness sake, and didn't need someone to remind her to pay her bills. Well, she didn't need *two* people, she amended, thinking of her assistant Tiffany.

Trying to tap into that more logical side of herself she'd only recently gotten used to using, she took a deep breath and tried to ignore the fresh cleanliness of the sheets she'd ensconced herself in and how much they reminded her of how Austin smelled.

Why not just enjoy it? said a quiet voice in the back of her mind. *Don't make plans, just have fun.*

Making out while Austin was in town didn't have to be the start of something major. It didn't mean they had to get married or anything. It could just be kissing, not the end of their worlds as they knew them.

She just needed to be careful not to let her stupid heart get involved. She needed to keep it in check so that it wasn't completely broken when this inevitably went south—or rather, when Austin went back west.

Her twenty-two-year-old love-struck self deserved some happiness, but that didn't mean twenty-six-year-old Harper had to be an idiot.

Satisfied with her plan, she took a deep breath and threw off the covers.

———

AUSTIN STARED into the crackling fire, the shifting rhythm of its flame soothing his anxious nerves.

He'd done it. He'd actually kissed her. Laid himself bare and told her everything. No plan, no clue what to do, he'd just gone for it.

And she'd run away.

If this was what she'd felt like at graduation when he'd done the same, then he was the biggest jerk in the world.

He was in the middle of calculating how much time it would take for him to walk back to the highway, and if it would be enough time for his embarrassment and shame to fade to manageable levels, when the bedroom door cracked open. Harper poked her head out, her still damp hair sticking up in every direction.

She was so beautiful, and he'd hurt her so much. Kept hurting her. The only reasonable plan here was to remove himself completely from her life, for real this time, and let her live in peace. He opened his mouth to tell her he'd be out of her hair soon when—

"I'm sorry I ran."

He looked at her in surprise. "You have nothing to be sorry for. I'm the one who ran all those years ago."

She shook her head. "You've already apologized for and explained that. I know how you are with surprises and, well, I did kind of lay a giant one on you. I forgive you. Really."

His heart soared at the words. Ok, so *Wedding Games* was probably ruined, and he'd never be allowed to work with Bruce again, but for Austin, this whole disaster of a week was worth it to have heard those words from Harper.

"I think that deserves a make-up kiss."

Her lips twitched. "It…" She looked around the room. The fire crackled happily, but she frowned. "What happened to the lights?"

Huh, he hadn't noticed either. "I guess the power went out while we were, ah…"

"Catching up?" The half-smile that slid across her face made his breath catch in his throat.

She walked over to him and grabbed his hand. Austin tried but failed not to overanalyze what that small gesture meant. She'd forgiven him, and they'd kissed, so were they together now? Should he ask to make it official? Could he put his arm around her?

He had so many questions, but his growling stomach beat him to the punch.

"Hungry?"

He chuckled. "All this running around hasn't exactly been conducive to eating."

"Hmm." She bit her lip. "Let's see what Eli's parents have hiding in the cabinets."

Austin watched her as she walked over to the kitchen, and started opening doors and drawers. She pulled a box down, and turned to him with a frown. "All I can find is this box of instant oatmeal. Not a lot to work with."

Austin stood up and walked to where she stood. He grabbed the box from her hand. "We can make oatmeal over a fire."

She made a face. "Sounds delicious."

"It could be worse." He laughed again and pointed to the fire. "Why don't you stay warm, and I'll take care of dinner."

As he prepared a very unappetizing but nourishing pot of oatmeal, they talked. And talked. And talked.

It was just like it had been in college. Maybe slightly less outright teasing, and a bit more cautious around certain topics, but this could have been any random Thursday night in her dorm room, chatting about their week.

It got even more reminiscent of college when Austin asked what she'd been watching lately. A completely normal question four years ago that drew an odd reaction out of Harper.

"Oh, I don't really have much time for TV these days," she said, but avoided his eyes.

He folded his arms across his chest. "Just tell me."

"I don't know what you mean." She was squirming uncontrollably from her seat by the fire, eyes on her hands.

"Is it that *Full House* reboot?"

She bit her lip. *"Hart of Dixie."*

Austin groaned. "And here I was actually worried about you being mad at me."

She grabbed a pillow from the couch and whacked him with it. "Hey, I get one pass after sitting through *Taken 3* with you."

He shrugged. "Liam Neeson is my spirit animal."

She laughed and eventually, they made their way to the couch, and Harper snuggled into his arms. It was a familiar position, one they'd taken a hundred times while watching a movie late into the night, but tonight, it felt different. It felt like the start of something new. The beginning of a new story for them. And this time, Austin planned to make sure he did everything right.

THIRTEEN

4 Days Until Dream Wedding

AUSTIN WOKE up early the next morning; his internal clock made it impossible to sleep past six. He slowly adjusted to his surroundings. He was in a dark cabin, sitting up on a couch, with Harper's head resting on a pillow in his lap.

The memories of the night before came rushing back. He'd kissed Harper. And she'd kissed him back. And—miraculously—she'd forgiven him for leaving her four years ago, and they'd spent the rest of the night talking.

Austin didn't remember falling asleep, but his body certainly felt the aches and pains that came with sleeping upright. He tried to shift in his spot, not wanting to wake Harper. But eventually the cramp in his lower back and the overwhelming urge to pee won, and Austin carefully slid out from under Harper's head and readjusted the pillow.

He held his breath as she mumbled something and turned her body to face the back of the couch. When her gentle snore interrupted the silence of the cabin,

Austin let out a relieved sigh and went to take care of his more pressing duties.

Once he was done, he went back to the couch with every intention of scooting beside Harper again. But he pulled up short at the sight of her sleeping so peacefully. The stress lines he'd seen grow deeper over the past twenty-four hours had finally smoothed out, and her entire body radiated calm. Had he done that? Happiness filled his chest, and he had to take a few deep breaths before he could move again.

Once again, his bodily needs interrupted his thoughts. Thirst finally overcame his overwhelming desire to stare at Harper all morning. He found a small cup in a cabinet and got a drink. He downed the water, then paced back and forth in the kitchen, replaying the kiss over and over again in his mind.

During college, Austin had kissed a lot of girls. With a pang, he realized he'd told Harper about them over Chinese food and reruns of *Parks and Rec*. He'd never experienced a kiss like the one last night though. If he'd known being with Harper would be like that…

He slammed his cup down on the kitchen counter. He'd been such an idiot when he'd graduated college. Deep down he'd known how good things would be with Harper, and he'd blown it anyway. But that didn't mean he had to repeat his mistakes.

Now that he was lucky enough to get a second chance with the girl he'd been in love with for years, he was going to do things right. And that meant helping her find Audrey.

He pulled out his phone, and his relief that he had a signal again quickly turned to panic. The screen was lit up with missed calls and a million texts from Jennifer that started last night and continued through the morning. The last one had just come through a few minutes earlier.

Where are you? You know your walkie is out of range?

Bruce is asking about you, and I can only stall so much.

Something weird is going on with the bride's family, and I can't quite put my finger on it. I need your help.

Please stop ignoring me.

The familiar churning of Austin's stomach at the thought of everything blowing up in his face was accompanied by the heart-wrenching hopelessness of his situation. He needed a plan, and the longer he stayed here, the more likely it was that he'd just curl up next to Harper and sleep the day away. Austin shoved the phone back in his pocket, and with one last lingering look at Harper, he walked out the front door.

—

HARPER STRETCHED OUT HER ARMS, waking up slowly. Her neck hurt for some reason, but she felt refreshed. She couldn't remember the last time she'd slept so peacefully.

All at once, the events of the previous night came flooding back to her.

Her broken down car.

The cabin.

Austin.

The kiss.

She'd fallen asleep the second she'd laid her head on

the pillow in Austin's lap. And while her head still rested on the pillow, Austin wasn't there anymore. Harper shot up from the couch and looked around. She wasn't sure if the power was back on, but the sun was just rising over the horizon, and she could easily see around the small cabin.

"Austin?" She held her breath. When he didn't reply, she called out again. "Hello? Are you here?"

Still nothing. Harper ignored the growing unease that filled her mouth with a dry, bitter taste like pure cocoa powder and got up from her spot on the sofa to look around. She checked the kitchen, the bathroom, and the porch. She called out for Austin every so often, and she was met with silence every time.

After searching for way too long in what was a relatively small cabin, Harper had to accept that the guy she'd spent the night pouring her heart out to—like she was a silly, trusting freshman—was nowhere to be found. Austin was gone.

"Don't panic." She swallowed the lump in her throat and grabbed her phone. Maybe he'd left a message for her. Her heart fluttered to see there was a signal again, and ten messages. But when she unlocked the screen, all she saw were a bunch of worried texts from Sienna.

Nothing from Austin.

Hot, embarrassing shame coursed through her. Harper *knew* it had been smart not to let Austin all the way back in. He had his grand plans, and they had nothing to do with her. They'd had one perfect kiss and spent one night together talking and he disappeared first thing in the morning to get back to his real life. His job was clearly more important than whatever stolen time they'd managed together.

Whatever. It didn't matter. He was gone, and that was fine. That was her plan, too. Have fun while it lasted, then things go back to the way they were before Austin and *Wedding Games* had crashed into her perfectly nice life.

The only thing she wondered about was how he got back to The Emerald Inn. Maybe he called that cute girl Jennifer he worked with, and she was able to bring him back.

Harper grabbed her things. Sadness and regret bubbled up that things hadn't lasted longer than a single night, but she pushed that away.

"Perfect," she mumbled when she slipped on her shoes that were still wet from the night before. Tears prickled in the corners of her eyes, and she swallowed hard to push them away.

She'd cried about Austin enough already in her life.

It was easy enough to tidy up the cabin since they hadn't really used much except the blankets and a pot for the oatmeal. Austin would have done a much better job of cleaning, but he wasn't here, was he? She locked up the cabin and started walking down toward the car. The ground was still damp, and she walked slowly to avoid slipping. The trek the day before had taken forever in the rain with Austin there to keep her from falling; it seemed twice as long on her own.

Finally, she saw her car exactly where she left it. She doubted it would work, but she had to try anyway. She reached into her purse and came up empty.

Oh, no. Did I leave them in the cabin?

The idea of hiking back up there in soggy shoes made Harper want to cry. But she'd already decided there'd be no crying this morning.

She dumped the contents of her bag on the hood of her car. "Where are my keys?"

Her head snapped up at the sound of crunching twigs. There, jingling a set of keys, was Austin. On his face was a big, stupid grin. "Looking for these?"

Harper stomped over and snatched them from his hand, and his smile fell. "What were you doing with them? Trying to make your escape?"

"What? No." His brow furrowed. "You thought I was leaving?"

She kept her face blank and shrugged, but her heart gave an involuntary leap. It went into full-on high-speed mixer levels when he wrapped his arms around her.

Simmer down now. He's leaving for real in four days.

"I didn't mean to worry you."

"You didn't," she said, and reluctantly pushed out of his warm embrace. "But, you know, notes are nice. And I got all these text messages from Sienna, so our phones work again."

He shook his head. "It was really spotty service in the cabin. I walked down to the freeway to get a stronger signal and call AAA. The mechanic just left."

Harper looked down at the keys in her hand. "The car works again?" She jogged over to her car and slid into the driver's seat. When she turned the key in the ignition, the engine roared to life.

A giddy laugh escaped her throat, and she looked out the windshield to see Austin smiling at her. Harper tried to tell herself the shiny happiness warming every part of her was because the car worked, and not because Austin was looking at her like she made the sun rise.

FOURTEEN

4 Days Until Dream Wedding

DESPITE AUSTIN'S reassurance that he could handle the curves, Harper had once again insisted on driving. Which meant she'd had only a minute to send a message to her younger sister before Austin threatened to wrangle the steering wheel from her.

On my way. Didn't find anything. Keep my return low key pls.

As if Sienna had ever done anything low-key in her life.

"Where were you?" Sienna's welcoming screech instantly alerted the entire *Wedding Games* crew of Harper's arrival.

Before she was even halfway up the winding gravel path that led from the parking lot to the inn, Sienna rushed down and almost tackled Harper to the ground with her hug.

"Hey," Harper said, suddenly worried. "I'm here. What happened?"

There were tears streaming from Sienna's eyes. "Fox

and I got into this huge fight and then I threw a plate, and now Marcey says she won't make me breakfast…"

Harper let out a secret sigh of relief. Sienna was still playing the part from yesterday. The heartbroken beauty would get a lot more attention than a missing sister. Or two.

"I should have brought some éclairs from the bakery. The oven is fixed, by the way, thanks for asking."

Sienna's brow furrowed then smoothed out when she understood the new element in their increasingly elaborate lie. Tiffany's single succinct text message had been mixed in with Sienna's ten rambling ones that Harper had received overnight. Apparently all it took was one call to the bakery to convince the producer that the emergency level of all four Flour Girl ovens breaking the same night meant Harper would be away until the morning. The show Sienna and Fox had put on must have been quite something for her to get away with being gone almost twenty-four hours without so much as a second glance.

Harper wondered what Austin had told the crew. He'd walked up ten minutes after her, so that it wouldn't be too obvious they'd arrived together. She looked around and spotted him near the equipment tent, and caught his eye. His face was blank, but he tilted his head up the tiniest bit, and she felt the same rush of warmth to her face that she'd been battling the whole drive back. Her forehead tingled at the spot where he'd planted a quick kiss before she'd gotten out of the car.

"What are you looking at?" Sienna whispered, her arm around Harper's shoulder. They were walking up to the inn, letting the cameras capture however much they wanted of this sisterly reunion. Hopefully enough they wouldn't realize there was still one sister missing.

"Nothing," Harper whispered back, but she couldn't tear her eyes away. She let her gaze linger on Austin for another minute. Just when she was about to focus on Sienna's fake disaster, someone came running up to him.

Harper's heart almost stopped when she realized it was Jennifer, the production assistant Austin had said he'd worked with before. The pretty one. She was just a friend. He'd said that, right?

But she was hugging him an awful lot like Harper wanted to.

Harper took a deep breath and focused on the inn. Reagan was coming out the front door and looked just as distraught as Sienna.

"Hey, I'm fine," said Harper, when Reagan put her arms around her.

"I know. It's just been a long day."

Harper pulled back to look at Reagan's tear streaked face. Was this all for the cameras? Or was Reagan upset for real? The unofficial Hudson sister wasn't nearly the actress as Sienna, and Harper worried that there was even more drama going on that she wasn't aware of. She was afraid to ask Reagan what was going on for fear of giving something away.

"Tell me about it," Harper said a little too loudly, earning a scowl from Sienna. "I've had the longest night trying to fix my ovens."

Reagan looped her arm through Harper's. "You simply must tell me all about it."

"Yes, I'd love to hear the story too," said Sienna, taking Harper's other arm.

Harper was led into the inn by the two women, and

she was grateful for the distraction from the brunette hanging off Austin. She couldn't help one last look back, however, and her stomach dropped at the sight of the two of them practically cheek to cheek as they looked at a clipboard.

It doesn't matter.

Harper had a big sister to find. As much as she hated that she had wasted an entire day and hadn't found her, maybe with Sienna and Reagan's help, they'd figure something out.

She'd had fun in the cabin, now her Austin distraction was officially over.

———

BRUCE WAS MAD. Austin could see it in the way the producer stalked around, barking out orders.

Well, he always stalked around and barked out orders, but this morning there was an edge to his movements that radiated a barely contained rage.

Austin hung back and waited until the producer stormed into the inn before he slipped into the tent. No one noticed besides Jennifer, who hugged him like he'd just come back from war. It was kind of nice to feel appreciated by someone on the crew, but her bushy brown curls blocked his view of Harper.

He pulled away quickly. "Hey, everything is fine. Just a flat tire."

"That took all night to fix?" Jennifer's eyes narrowed. She lowered her voice and leaned close to him and lay a finger on his clipboard, as if checking something with him. "I did what I could to cover for you, but Bruce is pissed. He wants to see you."

Austin's stomach disappeared and reappeared somewhere near his ankles. "When?"

"He said 'as soon as that good for nothing kid gets back, send him my way.'" Jennifer gave him a small, supportive smile. "Good luck with the beast."

Austin groaned. He'd much rather be spending his morning with the beauty he'd left behind in the parking lot.

It wasn't hard to find the producer. Austin just followed the sound of irritated yelling and ended up in the kitchen. He smiled when he thought of his time in there with Harper, but all happy feelings were quashed when he walked in to see Marcey and Bruce standing face to face, their faces red.

"You're in breach of contract!" he bellowed.

Anyone else would have cowered at that, but the young chef just put her hands on her hips and glared at him. "Show me where in my contract I'm supposed to let people smash up my kitchen." Her voice was quiet, but her eyes blazed.

"We need breakfast."

"I need plates to serve you breakfast. But the people on your show thought it would be loads of fun to throw them at each other."

"Surely, Sienna didn't destroy them all."

Sienna? Austin was dying to know what kind of disasters Harper's sister had caused the day before but held his tongue.

The small woman straightened her shoulders. "She shouldn't have destroyed any of them. Now I'm out of plates, you're out of breakfast, and we're both out of luck."

Bruce's face turned impossibly redder. Marcey

looked like she was ready to murder him and bake him into a pie. It would be suicide to get between the two of them, but that's exactly what Austin had to do.

He cleared his throat. "Uh, sir? You wanted to see me?"

Bruce whirled to face him, and he shrank back. "When did you get here?"

"A while ago." Staying vague would be safest in this situation.

"Well come on, I haven't got all day." Bruce stormed out, not even bothering to look at Marcey.

Austin gave a small shrug and hurried "sorry" to the chef, knowing it wouldn't be enough to fix whatever Sienna had done in an effort to cover for Audrey.

One crisis at a time, he reminded himself and he followed Bruce into the hall.

Bruce's big, hulking form leaned against the wall, arms crossed, and his gaze fixed on the ceiling.

"Care to explain your whereabouts the past eighteen hours?"

Bruce's voice was soft, and Austin almost wished he was shouting. He knew what to do with a mad Bruce, but this calm, quiet Bruce was way more dangerous. Austin had to tread carefully, like disarming a bomb.

His entire life felt like that for the past four years. Always on the edge of something exploding on him. Nothing seemed stable. That's why he always knew what to do, why he always had a plan. He'd started this job with page upon page of preparation for whatever the weather or the cast could throw his way.

But he'd never expected Harper. Spending the past day with her had completely thrown him off his carefully laid out path to a career he'd wanted for as long as he could remember. Choosing his own path instead of the one his parents had wanted for him had only been possible because he knew exactly what he needed to do every step of the way. Yet his time with Harper had felt more stable and more like the right choice than anything he'd done in years.

Austin knew that he needed to put in the work to get where he wanted to go. He'd already worked his way up the ladder rung by rung. Once he got just a little bit higher, he'd have enough contacts and experience to try things his way. Bailing on a production like he'd done the past day was like letting go of the ladder completely and starting from the bottom. But he wanted this, so badly. Dealing with Bruce's temper was just part of what needed to be done.

Though, right now, Austin would much rather be dealing with the debacles caused by Harper's reassuringly chaotic approach to life. And that was a serious problem. How could he finish work on the show when all he wanted to do was run to her room and watch TV with her all day?

"I'm sorry," Austin said, unsure of what else to say. It didn't seem like enough, but it was a start.

"Sorry won't get you far in this business, kid," said Bruce, and he turned his steely gaze to Austin's face. He didn't look disappointed or even angry. He looked completely unconcerned, which was so much worse.

"It won't happen again."

"You won't have the chance to let it happen again."

Austin's heart almost stopped. Was this really the end? Getting fired by Bruce wasn't just falling off the ladder, it was being pushed an ocean away from it. No one would want to hire Austin, even if they knew how awful Bruce was to work with.

The thought filled him with molten dread. What would he tell his parents? They'd only just started to recover from the blow that he went to film school instead of medical school. What would he tell Harper? He almost laughed. Maybe he could ask her for a job in her bakery.

Inspiration suddenly struck.

"I was working on an idea," Austin said. There was a breathless moment when Bruce considered him. When he nodded once, Austin let out all the air in his lungs in a whoosh. "The bakery. We could do a final competition between the bridesmaids and groomsmen."

Bruce was shaking his head. "We already had the s'mores contest."

"This would be a cake decorating contest. You know people are obsessed with baking competitions right now. I was making sure the ovens were okay at the bakery for us to do it."

"You're telling me that you started working on this? That you talked to Harper about it before consulting me?"

"I didn't want to waste your time unless I knew it would work." It was a great excuse. Bruce was always complaining about everyone wasting his time.

He considered Austin. "And Harper agreed to let us film there?"

"Yes." The lie flew out of Austin's mouth without hesitation. That was the first rule he'd learned as a production assistant: say yes to everything and figure out the details later. Besides, this would be a way to keep his job *and* spend more time with Harper.

It was brilliant, really. Austin crossed his fingers that Bruce would agree to it.

"Well…" The producer rubbed his chin. "That could work. We can't do it here since the chef is out of control. But we can't do it without the bride, and apparently, she's still sick."

"Oh?" Austin kept his face blank. "No updates?"

"I think she's made a run for it, personally. But that actress sister of hers keeps insisting she's just buried in her bed clutching a bucket. Until I see it, I won't believe it."

Austin continued to rack his brain. He needed Bruce to agree to this to take the pressure away from Audrey. "It can be just the bridesmaids and groomsmen. Like a surprise for the bride."

Bruce rubbed the bridge of his nose and sighed. "Fine. Take a couple people and a cameraman and make it work." Bruce dropped his hand and leveled Austin with a hard stare. "But this is it, Austin. Either this succeeds, or you're never going to work in television again."

Austin's nerves were strung so tightly that the cliché words from Bruce were almost enough to make him explode into a fit of laughter. Instead, he bit the inside of his cheek and gave Bruce a curt nod.

Bruce waved at him in dismissal, and Austin was happy to turn his face away as he walked down the hallway.

Now all he needed to do was find Harper and convince her to let Bruce use the Flour Girl Bakery for the competition that seemed to be tearing her family apart.

No problem.

FIFTEEN

4 Days Until Dream Wedding

HARPER DRAWLED on and on and *on* about the ovens at her bakery. And she still wasn't able to shake the cameraman who trailed behind the three girls. When she couldn't think of anything else to say—because honestly, there was only so much *to* say about ovens— she moved on to the mixer she wanted to order. And then the upcoming wedding cake that she'd worked on, careful to leave out the fact that Austin was with her when she had done the crumb coat.

Man, that felt like a hundred years ago, and it had been less than a day. It was baffling how much had happened in the time that she and Austin had been off The Emerald Inn's property, and she was dying to talk to someone about it.

"Well," she said, slowing down in front of her room. "After being in the kitchen all night, I think I'm ready to take a shower."

She held her breath as she unlocked the door to her room, hoping that the cameraman wouldn't follow her in.

"That sounds like a great idea," Sienna said. "I've been busy taking care of Audrey, and I really don't want to get sick. I think I'm going to go to my room and take a quick shower too."

She casually walked down the hall toward her room. Harper watched her sister disappear out of sight and was surprised that she hadn't turned to give her a sly wink or anything indicating that they were silently scheming together. But, that was what made Sienna the better actress. She fully committed herself to a role. Just ask Marcey's plates.

Barely able to keep herself from running down the hall to get the full story from Sienna, Harper opened the door. "What about you, Reagan?"

Her friend shrugged. "I don't know. Do you mind if I hang out and watch TV in your room while you get cleaned up? Harry is...resting, and I don't want to disturb him."

"Sure," Harper answered, and risked a look at the cameraman who still stood in the hall. "You coming?"

The question rolled off her tongue easily, and she even managed to sound bored, though that was the furthest from how she actually felt. Her heart pounded as she struggled to keep her face impassive.

The cameraman lingered for a moment, and Harper pushed her luck by raising a haughty brow at him. He rolled his eyes and shook his head. "Nah. I'm going to see if I can get any interesting footage of the guys."

Harper shrugged. "Suit yourself."

But the second he started walking in the opposite direction, she pulled Reagan inside the room and shut the door behind them. She plopped on the bed and let out a long, shaky breath. "Thank goodness. I wasn't sure what I was going to do if he decided to come in."

"You could start talking about your mixing bowls since now I officially know everything there is to know about your ovens." Reagan smiled but didn't meet Harper's eyes.

"Do you want to tell me what's really going on?"

"You mean about Sienna? The fight wasn't real, I thought you knew that?"

Harper folded her arms and peered at Reagan. "I do know that. But I want to know why you looked like you'd been crying when you first came up to me. And why you lied and told the cameraman that Harry was resting."

Reagan bit her bottom lip and stared out the window. "I don't really want to talk about it."

Harper got up and walked over to Reagan and wrapped her arms around her. "Are you sure?"

"Yeah. It's nothing anyway. I'm dying to know what's going on with the bakery and Audrey and—"

Loud knocking on the door interrupted Reagan, and both girls' eyes went wide. It would be just Harper's luck if the cameraman had changed his mind and come back to film in hopes of picking up some secret drama. Secret drama Reagan had almost revealed to Harper.

The knocking came again. "Quick. Let me in!"

Harper smiled as she recognized Sienna's voice and ran over to the door.

"It took you long enough. Do you know how many secret agent moves I had to pull out to make sure I wasn't spotted when I came back around to your room?"

"Sorry," Harper said as she locked the deadbolt. "I was afraid the cameraman changed his mind."

"Well, he didn't. But who knows how long we have before someone comes looking for us." Sienna sat down in the chair in the corner of the room while Harper and Reagan took seats on the bed. "So, dish. What happened last night? And what's the real reason you didn't come home?"

"I was looking for Audrey."

"And you just, I don't know, decided it would be fun to give your other sister an evening long panic attack?" Sienna threw up her hands. "I was so worried. I didn't know where you were, and you weren't answering your phone."

"I got stuck at Eli's cabin. There wasn't any reception."

Reagan perked up from her spot beside Harper. "What were you doing up there?"

"Austin—" Harper cleared her throat. "The production assistant and I went up hoping Audrey would be there."

Sienna's eyes were as wide as saucers. "You spent the night at the cabin with *Austin?*" His name came out as a song, and Harper was afraid Sienna might start singing about them hiding in a tree k-i-s-s-i-n-g.

"It wasn't like that. My car broke down, and it started storming." She touched the ends of her hair realizing she probably looked like a complete disaster. Even though she'd been able to take a shower, the cabin only had two-in-one shampoo and conditioner that did nothing for her hair. And she'd gone without lotion, which meant her face felt stiff and dry.

Meanwhile, Sienna and Reagan looked as perfect as usual. Just like that Jennifer girl who had run over to

Austin the second he'd gotten back. Did everyone have to look like a supermodel all of the time?

Reagan bumped Harper's shoulder with her own. "I think that Austin guy is pretty cute. There are worse people to be stuck in a cabin with overnight."

"He's okay." *And an amazing kisser.*

"Okay?" Sienna asked with a raised eyebrow. "If I wasn't head-over-heels for Fox, I might flirt a little with him."

A flare of jealousy sparked in Harper's veins. She loved Sienna, but her sister was exactly the type of girl Austin always dated in college. Even if she wasn't going to let this thing with Austin get serious, the idea of the guy she'd been in love with for years flirting with Sienna made her want to scream.

"But Harper isn't dating anyone," Reagan said. "She really could flirt with Austin."

Too late.

"And maybe she could get some intel while we try to find Audrey," Sienna added. "What do you think, Harper?"

Harper forced a smile. "Sure. I guess I could talk to him."

"Great." Sienna crinkled up her nose. "But you might need to clean up for real before trying to talk to him. I don't know what you got into last night, but you are smelling ripe."

Harper lifted her arm and took a quick whiff. "Ugh. You're right. Okay. I'm going to take a quick shower."

"I'm going to sneak back to my room before anyone gets suspicious." Sienna got up from the chair. "Just let me know if I need to fight with Fox anymore."

"You mean break some more dishes?" Harper smirked.

Sienna smiled sweetly. "I don't know what you're talking about."

Harper snorted. "Marcey was pissed."

"What can I say? I'm the overly dramatic one. Every single cameraman was following me hoping to catch what I'd do next. I couldn't disappoint them." Sienna's smile was bright, but Harper could hear a hint of sadness in her voice.

"I'm sorry. I know how much you wanted to be seen as a serious actress."

"Actor," Sienna corrected.

"*Actor*," Harper said. "I know that must have been really hard."

Her sister shrugged. "What was I supposed to do? Let Bruce find out Audrey is gone and ruin everything?"

"No. But it still means a lot."

"I know. And we'll find her. You'll see."

Harper really hoped so. Between Audrey's disappearance, Bruce's attitude, keeping Flour Girl afloat during filming, and whatever was happening with Austin, Harper was dangerously close to losing it. If at least one of her problems could be resolved, she may actually manage to breathe easy for a minute or two. She closed her eyes and massaged her temples.

"And what should I do?"

Reagan's hopeful voice made Harper look up. She didn't know, and she didn't want to be the one responsible for it anymore. She lifted a shoulder. "Keep covering for Audrey?"

Reagan's face fell. "Yeah, okay."

"I know it's not a fun job." She started to put her

arm around her friend but thought better of it when she remembered the way she smelled. Instead, she grabbed Reagan's hand. "Hopefully we'll find her today and we can stop sneaking around."

"I hope so."

"Harper is going to flirt with the production hottie and see what she can find out." Sienna led Reagan toward the door. "And this whole thing will blow over by dinner."

Harper wasn't convinced but didn't argue. She didn't have the energy. So she lifted her hand in a weak wave as the two girls walked out of her room and into the hallway. Finally, she was alone with her thoughts.

It only took about two seconds before they inevitably went back to Austin, the "production hottie" she was now tasked with flirting with for information about what the crew suspected. She almost burst out laughing at the irony of it but settled for a slightly deranged giggle from her place on the bed.

What would Sienna and Reagan think if they knew she'd spent the night kissing Austin instead of looking for Audrey? What would they think if they knew she'd known him for what felt like forever and been in love with him all these years?

They'd be the ones laughing at her for thinking he would ever do more than flirt with her. Whatever Austin and Harper had was never going to last more than one night.

But Audrey still had to be found, even if all Harper wanted to do was hide in her room until the wedding was over. So she turned on some music—loud enough to drown out all remaining thoughts of Austin—and got into the shower.

SIXTEEN

4 Days Until Dream Wedding

AUSTIN WAS STARTING TO PANIC. He couldn't find Harper anywhere.

He'd seen Sienna sneaking out the back door with Fox. He'd seen Reagan arguing with Harry in one of the hallways. He'd seen more cameramen swarming around than he had all week. But everywhere he looked, there was no sign of Harper.

He was going to go check the kitchen again, and face Marcey's wrath, when he bumped into Jennifer.

Her mouth fell open as their eyes met down the hall from each other, and she came racing over. "Oh, thank goodness. I didn't hear anything or see you after you talked to Bruce, and I was sure you were already gone on the first flight back to LA."

Austin shook his head and bounced on the balls of his feet. He was anxious to keep looking for Harper. He had to figure out how to convince her to host the baking competition, but he also needed to keep his cool around Jennifer. She was smart, and it was a miracle she hadn't called him out on his crap yet.

He lifted a corner of his mouth into what he hoped was a casual, slightly arrogant smile. It was everything he didn't feel right now. "You know Bruce wouldn't pay for a flight back. I'd be hitchhiking the entire way."

"Good point." Jennifer giggled. "I'm just happy you're still here."

Me too. Though for very different reasons.

"What did Bruce say when you went to see him?"

Austin forced his hands to stay relaxed at his side even though they itched to touch his face or tap the clipboard. "He's worried about Audrey's illness lasting as long as it is."

"You mean her supposed illness." Jennifer smirked. "That girl isn't sick, and everyone knows it."

Austin's eyes went wide.

"Oh, come on. You're not that green. The bride's got cold feet, and her sisters think we're dumb enough to buy the act. It's insulting, really." She sniffed and looked at her bright pink fingernails.

"Well, either way, Bruce needs some footage to keep things moving."

Jennifer took a step toward him. "And?"

"I think we have the perfect solution. We're going to do a cake decorating competition."

She let out a long breath and rolled her eyes. "Does he really think another competition is going to save the show?"

"It, uh, was my idea."

"Oh." She paused a beat, then smiled. "Great idea!"

"I figured baking shows are such a hit, it was worth a shot. And since Harper has the bakery—"

"Harper." Jennifer's lips pressed together in a hard

line. "The girl you went to college with. The girl you supposedly don't really know."

"I told you, I don't." He hated the way the lie felt on his tongue, but what was he supposed to do? He couldn't tell Jennifer what was really going on between him and Harper. Not with so much on the line. Not with Austin's career on such thin ice.

Jennifer stared at him intently. "Whatever. I'm stuck doing coffee runs since the chef won't let anyone near the kitchen. I'll see you later."

Ugh. Austin would take that over his current predicament any day. "Yeah. I'll let you know when I know more about the competition."

Jennifer gave him one more strange look before she continued down the hallway.

With a sigh of relief, Austin walked in the opposite direction toward the kitchen. He was just about to go inside—maybe Harper had gone back to drool over the mixer some more—when he saw Sienna speed walking down the hall.

"Hey," he called out.

Sienna stopped in her tracks, and slowly turned her head toward him.

"Have you seen Harper?"

A smile spread across her lips. "Why are you looking for my sister?"

"I need to talk to her. About show stuff."

Sienna raised an eyebrow but said nothing.

He let out an impatient huff. "Do you know where she is or not?" Austin did not have time for Harper's drama queen little sister right now.

"She's getting cleaned up after last night's escapade."

Wait. How much did Sienna know?

"I bet if you ran up there now, she'd still be in her room."

There was a sly smirk on her lips that Austin wasn't sure how to interpret, but he wasn't going to stay there overanalyzing everything until he lost his chance.

Without a word, he raced down the hall, up the stairs to Harper's room, all while keeping an eye out for cameras, co-workers, and especially Bruce.

Out of breath, he knocked on the door.

"What did you forget this—" The door swung open and Austin came face to face with a wide-eyed Harper. "What are you doing here?"

He cleared his throat and wiped his palms on his pants. "I, uh…"

Harper reached out and grabbed the front of his shirt and pulled him inside. She slammed the door and spun to face him. "Are you insane? You know we can't be seen together."

"Actually," Austin said. "Bruce knows I'm here. He's starting to get suspicious about Audrey and sent me to find you."

Her eyes went wide. "Oh, no. This is a disaster."

"It's not like that." He grabbed her hands but was surprised when she pulled them away and took a step back. He hurried to explain. "I convinced him to do another competition. It distracted him from Audrey."

Harper sighed and then began pacing the small room, not looking even the slightest bit relieved after what Austin had done for her. "Another one? I don't think I can handle anything else while we search for the missing bride."

Oh right. He'd left out the best part. "Even a baking one?"

She stopped, and a surge of victory pulsed through him. He knew how to get her attention.

"And I guess that means I need to be a part of it." She scowled.

Whoops, not that kind of attention. He tried again. "I thought it could be a win-win. You were so good during the s'mores competition. Maybe if you did a good job with the cake—"

"The cake! *That's* the baking competition?"

"Well, technically it's a cake decorating competition. You'd just need to make the cakes beforehand."

Harper sighed and her hands went to her temples.

Austin shifted on his feet, unsure of what to say. Harper had frosted that cake in her bakery like it was nothing.

"Austin, do you know what you're asking me to do?"

"Bake a few cakes?"

She threw her hands up in the air. "I've already got one wedding cake on the schedule, not to mention a business to keep running. Oh, and a missing sister. It's not like I can just whip up a dozen cakes in twenty minutes. It's not a store-bought roll of cookie dough."

He ran a hand through his hair. "I don't know what to tell you. Bruce was—" He stopped himself before he said "yelling at me" unwilling to let Harper see how much trouble he was in right now. He cleared his throat. "He was talking to me about what to do, and this was the first thing I could think of because I knew you'd be so good at it."

Harper's face softened a fraction. "You think so?"

Austin lifted a corner of his mouth. "Of course I do.

And once everyone sees how great you are, I bet the Flour Girl gets so much business. All the tourists will want to visit the famous Harper Hudson."

A slight blush hit Harper's cheeks. "I doubt it."

"Why wouldn't they?" Austin's smile grew, and he took a couple of steps closer to Harper. "Who knows, maybe you'll get your own baking show."

She laughed. "Could you imagine? Sienna would be so mad."

"And?"

"And it's not going to happen." She shook her head.

"The show? Or the competition?"

Harper looked up at Austin through lowered eyelashes. "I'll do the competition, but my own baking show isn't going to happen, and I think we both know that."

Austin deflated a little. She was right. She probably wouldn't get a show, but not because she wasn't talented enough to do it. The business was all about connections, and after the hell her family had put the crew through this past week, Bruce Bigg wasn't going to help Harper —or any Hudson—get a show even if his life depended on it.

"Regardless, I appreciate you being willing to do it."

"Anything for my sister." The small smile on her face nearly broke Austin's heart.

"And maybe when everything's said and done, you can give me a baking lesson."

She lifted her brows. "That could be...interesting."

Austin's heart lifted. "I mean, it's kind of far to California for just one lesson, so I'd expect at least three while you're out there."

"I'm coming to California, am I?" The corner of her mouth twitched.

"That's the plan." He had a plan. With Harper in it. All was right again in his world. "I mean, I want to see you again, when this is all over. But I could come here. Whatever you want."

A smile spread across her face. "It'll take more than three lessons to get you anywhere near a decent baker."

"Doesn't the crumb layer count as lesson number one? I'm totally ready for lesson number two."

She shoved his shoulder. "You're such a dork."

He chuckled. "Maybe. But that's what you love about me."

Harper sucked in a quick breath. It was a phrase that he'd said countless times as a joke to Harper back in college—before she'd confessed that she actually loved him.

But she hadn't said it since then. And Austin knew better than anyone not to push Harper into something she didn't want.

Austin took a deep breath. "Look, I—"

"What time do I need to be down in the kitchen for this thing?"

Austin froze.

Harper closed her eyes and sighed. "It's at Flour Girl, isn't it?"

She'd always been able to read his mind. "Yeah. Right after dinner."

Harper opened her eyes and glared at him. "Okay. Then let me call Tiffany and tell her to close down for the afternoon."

"Okay," Austin said and walked toward the door.

"I'll start getting the crew together and meet you at Flour Girl in an hour to get set up."

She nodded, but her eyes were focused on the door. No, not the door. He knew that look. Harper was somewhere far away.

"Hey." He took her by the arm. She shook her head and looked up at him, as if waking from a dream. "Don't worry. Audrey will be back. I promise."

I hope.

She gave him a smile, a real one this time, and he turned to open the door.

He got exactly one step out the door when he felt her hand on his back. It slid down and around his waist, her arms circling him from behind. They stayed like that for a few breathless moments, Harper's head on Austin's back, and her arms holding him tight.

"Thank you for having a plan," she whispered just before she leaned forward to kiss his cheek. "Thank you for not giving up on me."

"Always," he whispered back. Just as he was about to turn and kiss her the way he'd been wanting to since they got back to the inn, her hands slipped off of him, and the door closed behind him.

He scrubbed his hands across his face. There was so much to do today to prepare for the contest, but all he wanted to do was run back into her room and talk like they had last night. He sighed and dropped his hands. His stomach dropped right along with them when his eyes caught a movement down the hall.

Jennifer was at the end of the hallway, hands on her hips. She'd seen everything.

SEVENTEEN

4 Days Until Dream Wedding

*J*UST PLAY IT COOL. *Maybe she won't think it's a big deal.*

"What was *that?*" Jennifer asked when Austin finally made his way down the hall to her.

"What?" Austin shrugged and kept walking. "I had to talk to her about some set up stuff at the bakery."

"And that required her hands all over you?"

Austin stopped in his tracks and turned.

Jennifer's lips pursed together, and she tapped her foot in what he recognized as her irritated rhythm. He had two choices. Pretend nothing had happened, basically gas-lighting her by convincing her she was seeing things, or he could come clean and ask for her help. He knew which one Bruce would do, which one Austin had seen him do countless times. It worked every time, and got Bruce everything he wanted.

Austin knew he had to do the opposite.

"Ok fine, maybe we *did* know each other in college. We were friends," he said. "You're not going to say anything are you?"

"I covered for you because I thought you were stuck

somewhere with a flat tire or needed a break and went to a bar," she said, her eyes an icy blue. If Harper's gray ones were like a warm summer storm cloud, then Jennifer's were a freezing winter sky. "Not because you were off with a cast member who you knew before we started filming."

"I wasn't off with her, I was just with her looking for —" He stopped and took a breath. "Looking for some equipment I lost when we were filming the scavenger hunt. I thought it might be at her bakery. That's when I got the idea for the cake decorating competition."

It was close enough to the truth that it flowed from his mouth without hesitation.

Still, Jennifer raised an eyebrow.

"Are you going to tell him or not?"

She licked her lips. "That depends."

Austin leaned in close, hating that he was flirting with Jennifer just to make sure she didn't blab to Bruce. It was such a skeezy move. A Bruce move. And if he wasn't trying to protect Harper, he would confess the whole situation to the shrewd producer just so he didn't have to get cozy with Jennifer.

"I want you to take me out on a date."

Austin blinked. "What?"

She took a step toward him. "You heard me. I'm tired of waiting for you to wake up and realize I'm your perfect match. I want you."

"Um, doesn't Bruce hate the crew hooking up even more than when the crew gets with the cast?"

She waved away his concern. "I'm not saying make out with me in front of everyone at breakfast. But you know the crew can't be everywhere all the time. A quick walk out on the trails, a rendezvous in the barn."

"Jennifer…"

She placed her hand gently on his chest. "And once we're back in LA next week, you can take me on our first official date."

From the look on her face, she wanted a lot more than a date from him. He swallowed hard. "Look, you're great but—"

"And as my boyfriend, I'd obviously keep all your secrets for you." She fixed him with a calculating stare. "All of them."

Austin's breath caught in his throat. Did she suspect about Audrey? Man, he'd been such an idiot to almost let that slip. He could feel everything spinning out of control. But what choice did he have? If Jennifer said anything to Bruce about him and Harper, he'd be fired. He'd already used his one get-out-of-jail-free card with Bruce.

To convince Jennifer he was into her would mean ignoring Harper. He would have to break her heart. Again.

But it was the only way to save everything: Harper, her family, the show, and his career.

"Okay."

With a quiet squeal, Jennifer wrapped her arms around him and kissed him on the mouth before he could stop her.

THE MORNING HAD BEEN a blur of setting up cameras and equipment in the bakery, and Harper was ready for a nap. But there was no time, not when she had five cakes to bake for the competition.

"Why did it have to be wedding cakes?" she moaned to Tiffany, who was going above and beyond, yet again, this time by helping Harper mix up the batter.

"Would you rather be making five hundred cupcakes?"

Harper snorted. "No thank you. Once was enough." After the disastrous event the previous summer, when half the cupcakes had fallen to the floor, the Flour Girl Bakery only did wedding cakes. Harper knew she was missing out on a piece of the market, but there was only so much stress a person could handle in life. She drew the line at personalized cupcakes.

"When are the bridesmaids and groomsmen getting here?" Tiffany asked.

"Right now!" called a voice from the door.

The two women turned to see Reagan and Sienna walk into the kitchen.

Harper didn't know if she was relieved or pissed. "Put on a hairnet before you touch anything."

"But I just did my hair." Sienna stuck out her lower lip. "Besides, we're not here to help."

"Of course not," mumbled Harper.

Beside her, Tiffany giggled.

Louder, Harper asked, "So what are you doing here three hours early?"

"It was boring at the inn," said Reagan, perching on a stool in the corner, hands folded neatly in her lap. "And we wanted to hear how your secret mission went."

Harper cast a glance at Tiffany. "I think you've done enough overtime for one week. I can finish up. Thanks for all your help."

Tiffany looked like she wanted to argue, but she hung up her apron on a peg by the door and washed her hands before waving goodbye. Harper knew she'd be happy with the extra money, but she was also barely out of high school. The girl had a social life, unlike Harper whose only plans outside work had been her weekly Sunday afternoons with Audrey. Until this wedding had taken over everyone's lives, that is.

Despite the endless frustration caused by the reality show, thinking of her missing sister still made her stomach twist into knots.

"So what did you find out?" Sienna said eagerly, leaning over the work table, her long blond hair hanging over her shoulder.

"Sienna, I swear, if you get a single hair in these cakes, I will knock a tooth out."

The youngest Hudson sister rolled her eyes. "Calm down, they're just for the show, right? We won't be eating them or anything."

"Well, I take pride in my work. Would you only give half of your energy during a rehearsal so you could save it for opening night?"

Sienna clicked her tongue but backed off and took a seat next to Reagan. "Seriously, Harper, spill the details, we're dying over here."

Harper kept her eyes on the bowl of batter she was mixing a little too vigorously and shrugged. "He didn't say anything about Audrey, he just told me about this cake competition."

"You are the worst flirt ever, Harper," her sister whined. "I should have done it myself."

Harper huffed. "I'm sure Fox would just love that."

At the sound of his name, Sienna lit up from the inside. "He would understand. I wish you could have seen him yesterday. He was spectacular. He says he doesn't want to be a performer anymore, but I'd bet within a week of getting to New York he's going to more auditions than me."

Harper's eyebrows shot up. "He's going back to New York with you?"

"Of course. I'm not exactly made for life on a fishing boat."

"He'd just give up his whole life for you? Just like that?"

Sienna laughed. "It's not like working on boats was his big dream. It was just something he did to escape the life he thought he didn't want."

A tiny hole appeared in the little happy bubble that had been floating inside Harper ever since Austin had mentioned her visiting him. Of course she couldn't expect him to give up everything for her. Working in TV had been important to him for as long as Harper could remember. He'd defied his parents to move to LA, had worked himself to the bone to move up the precarious Hollywood ladder, and was now finally within reach of moving into something big through his work with Bruce. Why would he give up all that hard work for her?

Harper shook her head and grabbed the cake pans from the cabinet. She tried to ignore Reagan and Sienna's chatter as she poured in the batter with even, practiced movements. The familiar routine of balancing the heavy pans on her arms and placing them in the hot ovens was soothing. Austin wasn't Fox, and Harper definitely wasn't Sienna. What her sister's relationship looked like—both of her sisters—didn't define what hers had to be. She had her stolen moments and stolen kisses with him, that was enough for now.

"Anyway, Harper, what else did Austin say?" Sienna's question pulled Harper out of her thoughts.

"What? Nothing." She bit her tongue. Of course her voice would sound shaky now, of all moments.

Reagan raised an eyebrow but didn't comment. "He didn't say why they're doing this cake competition? Do they know Audrey's gone?"

"I don't think so, but Bruce is losing patience." Harper felt a flutter of panic run through her but pushed it down before it got too close to her head. This was not the moment to lose her cool. "If she doesn't show up today, I don't know how they'll be able to finish the show."

Reagan and Sienna exchanged a worried look.

"So what are we going to do?" asked Sienna.

Harper inhaled deeply. Her sister still expected her to have all the answers, even after failing to find Audrey. Harper had never felt so lost. So she did what she'd done when she was younger: rely on Austin's plan to get her through. "We're going to decorate cakes."

EIGHTEEN

4 Days Until Dream Wedding

"ALRIGHT, alright, welcome to the cake decorating competition."

Jason Castle's voice gave no hint that this was anything but a totally planned part of the show. Harper hoped her own face was just as convincing because when she looked around the room, everyone was in various states of agitation.

Reagan was looking at her hands, her red hair falling in her face. Harry was leaning against the counter, his arms crossed and eyes narrowed. Fox looked grumpy, but from what Harper had seen of him, that was his default mood. Only Wade and Sienna seemed to be just as unflustered as Harper was attempting to appear.

Sienna because she was such a good actress—*actor*, Harper corrected with a roll of her eyes—and Wade because he was just an easygoing guy. Harper held back a sigh. More than once Audrey had tried to push Harper toward Eli's friend, without much success. Wade was a great guy, but not for her.

A sharp pang of guilt shot through Harper when she

noticed Eli off to the side, worrying his bottom lip with his teeth. She hadn't even stopped to consider what the groom must be thinking right now. Had Fox told him that Audrey was sick or had he told him the truth? Eli would be worried either way, but only one scenario meant he wouldn't be getting married in four days.

Sienna nudged Harper, and she returned her attention to Jason, who was explaining the rules. "Each bridesmaid and groomsman will get a cake and unlimited access to the decorating supplies so kindly provided by the Flour Girl Bakery in Wellspring, North Carolina."

Harper bit the inside of her cheek to keep from scowling. "Unlimited" meant she'd be spending the next week restocking her supply. When someone had come by with a contract for Harper to sign earlier in the day, Austin had been nowhere to be found. She would have liked for someone to take the time to let her know what was in it, but she'd been too busy to do anything but sign it. She had at least scanned it briefly. There'd been some mention of remuneration in exchange for her providing the space and materials, but now she wondered if all that meant was Jason saying the name of her bakery.

"You all will get a brief introduction from Tiffany, head of decorating here at the bakery, and then will have an hour to complete your cakes."

Harper almost snorted, and she got a glare from Sienna. "Head of decorating" was a fake title she'd made up to get Tiffany to cancel her plans and come back to the bakery.

"The judge will be the groom himself, since this will serve as the traditional groom's cake."

"But won't Harper win anyway?" Harry turned his

eyes to Jason. "I mean, it's her bakery. She's a professional so why are the rest of us even trying?"

Jason's smile didn't even tremble. "That's the second part of this. Harper isn't participating as a contestant. She will spend ten minutes with each of you, lending her help however she can."

After a few more directions and smiles at the cameras, Jason wished them all good luck and stepped away. Tiffany replaced him at the front of the kitchen and demonstrated how to apply the crumb layer, make buttercream flowers, and—for those daring enough to attempt it—how to roll out and apply fondant.

Harper bit her tongue to keep from jumping in once or twice, but overall, her young assistant did really well —especially considering there were three cameras trained on her every move. Despite Austin's big dreams of Harper becoming a baking show superstar, she knew bubbly and bright Tiffany was much better suited for a life in front of the camera than her sarcastic and awkward boss.

When Tiffany was done, Wade and Sienna descended on the decorating supplies and started filling their arms with goodies like kids on Halloween. The others were more hesitant, their enthusiasm subdued.

"They need to be a little more interesting."

Harper jumped a little to hear Austin's voice in her ear. It was the first time she'd seen him all day, and a smile tugged at her lips. But it was wiped from her face the instant she turned and saw his face. She'd never seen Austin looking so serious. Or so angry. His eyebrows were drawn together so closely it was hard to tell that he had two. He'd leaned in close to whisper in her ear, but pulled back as soon as he'd given her the message.

"What am I supposed to do about it?" She hoped she sounded irritated and not disappointed. Of course he had to pretend not to know her, but this was a little extreme.

"Figure it out. The second Bruce gets bored, the questions about Audrey will start." Then he walked away.

He walked away!

Harper stood frozen in place, her heart pounding in her ears. What had happened between this morning and now that would make him treat her this way? Doubt rolled around in her stomach. He said he wanted her to visit. She hadn't made that up. Right?

Or maybe she'd just misunderstood. Maybe all he wanted was a baking lesson. Or maybe all he'd wanted was for her to agree to let him use the kitchen, and he'd do whatever it took for her to say yes.

A heavy pressure of tears built up behind Harper's eyes, and she blinked to keep them away. While crying on camera would certainly be interesting, it wasn't what Harper wanted Austin to see.

"Harper, are you okay?" Sienna asked. She was spreading frosting over her cake in giant globs.

"No." She looked over her shoulder. The cameramen weren't at Sienna's station yet, but they were walking toward them. "We need to be more interesting," she mouthed to Sienna quickly hoping her drama queen sister might be able to help.

Sienna winked so fast, Harper almost missed it, and then started scooping giant piles of frosting onto the cake.

When Sienna plopped the fifth heap on top, Harper snatched the large offset spatula out of her hand.

"You're ruining this poor cake."

"I'm not ruining it! More frosting is always better."

"It's too much. Just let me do it."

"No." Sienna pushed Harper out of the way and grabbed the spatula back. "You always think your way is the only way."

"Give it back." Harper swiped at the spatula, but Sienna held it behind her back.

"It's mine," she said, and feigned to the right before scooting the other way around the edge of the counter.

Harper hesitated for just a moment, threw up her hands like she was giving up, then lunged for Sienna.

The chase that ensued around the kitchen was met with delighted guffaws of laughter from Wade and Fox, and a few short bursts of cursing from the cameramen. Sienna flicked frosting behind her back, and a glob landed right on Harper's forehead.

"Get back here!"

"Never!"

Wade and Fox were shouting out encouragement, while Reagan simply stepped out of their path whenever they flew by, calmly frosting her cake in between these breaks. It could have gone on for hours—neither Harper nor Sienna liked to give in easily—but what finally got them to stop was the voice of Bruce booming over the chaos.

"That's enough for now."

They were both breathing heavily and leaned on the counter by Sienna's barely frosted cake. Harper felt proud that she and Sienna had pulled off something exciting, but when she snuck a glance at Austin, he looked unimpressed. He lifted his brows impatiently and jerked his head toward Reagan.

Harper couldn't understand why he was being so mean—even the crew members who didn't know her smiled a little when they talked to her—but she playfully nudged Sienna and walked over to where Reagan was rolling out fondant like a pro.

"Feel better?" Reagan asked with a playful smile.

"Gotta have a little fun, right?"

Reagan's eyes flicked briefly to where Harry was cussing at the frosting he smeared on his cake, and back to Harper. "Uh-huh."

"Do you want any help?"

Reagan shook her head, causing her red curls to bounce. "No, I think I'm okay. But you might want to go check on the boys before they destroy their cakes—and your bakery."

Harper followed Reagan's gaze and saw Wade rolling the fondant into something that didn't look appropriate for network television and gave Reagan a rushed goodbye before walking over to his space.

She smacked her hand on his creation, flattening the inappropriate sculpture. "What are you doing?" she hissed.

Wade shrugged unapologetically. "I figured you and Sienna shouldn't be the only ones having fun."

She smacked him. Hard.

But he only chuckled, a loud and deep rumble. "Remind me never to make you angry."

"And remind me never to give you something you can mold again."

"Did you come over to babysit me?" He gathered the smushed fondant and started rolling it into a ball.

"I get ten minutes with everyone, and I figure now is as good a time as any." She snatched the fondant back. "And I just saved us from getting fined by the FCC."

Wade eyeballed the ball of fondant before going for the buttercream. "The network would have been fined. Not us. But they would have blurred it out anyway."

"Better safe than sorry though."

"Speaking of sorry," Wade said. "If I ever get married, which I won't, I'd be really sorry to get a groom's cake covered in delicate fondant flowers. Aren't they supposed to be chocolate...and slightly more manly?"

Harper sighed. That was the same argument she made to one of the crew members when they gave her a list of items to have on hand. She'd wanted to talk to Austin about it, knowing he would understand and do his best to fix it, but she'd been afraid to hint at any relationship between the two of them.

Poor Austin. He must be so stressed out with the pressure of the show and keeping secrets from his boss. That was the only explanation for how snippy he'd been to her earlier. Harper's eyes went to him to see if he'd relaxed at all since the last time she'd snuck a glance. But Austin wasn't looking at her when she turned her head.

Harper's breath caught in her throat when she saw him next to Jennifer. He put a hand on her back and whispered in her ear. But instead of pulling away, like he had with Harper, he leaned in. Jennifer giggled and put her hand on his cheek and Austin's hand touched her waist. It was just for a second, and when Harper blinked, the two of them had separated and were on opposite sides of the camera, watching the contestants.

The floor vanished under Harper's feet. She gripped

the counter, steeling herself against the dizzy realization that everything had been a lie. This was a reality show, after all, so why was she surprised that the crew was so good at manipulation?

"Harper?" She felt a strong hand on her shoulder and looked up to see concern etched all over Wade's features. He gave her shoulder a slight squeeze. "You okay?"

That was the thing about Wade. He seemed totally aloof and never serious enough on the surface, but under his playful exterior, he was considerate and genuine. Why, oh why, couldn't Harper fall for someone like him? Probably because he felt too much like a sibling, like Reagan. It was the replacement family the Hudson sisters had created for themselves when their real one had begun to fall apart.

She cleared her throat. "Uh, yeah. Of course. Just thinking about how we should have done chocolate cake like you said."

He lifted a brow waiting for the truth.

But Harper didn't want to talk about the real reason she was upset. "Do you need any help with the frosting?"

Wade shook his head. "I think I'm good, and I promise not to do anything else to get anyone in trouble."

Harper leaned in and gave him a hug. "Thanks. I'm sure Bruce will appreciate that."

Harper continued to walk around the kitchen after that. No one wanted her instruction, and it was probably better that way anyway. Everyone was doing everything wrong, and it would have taken too much time to teach them the proper technique.

Not that she could have, even if she wanted to. Her thoughts were completely focused on Austin and Jennifer. Were they dating? Had they been dating this whole time? They looked awfully cozy. Probably whispering about how dumb Harper had been to believe anything Austin had told her.

Without meaning to, Harper ended up back at Sienna's station. Her cake looked a hot mess. The buttercream layer was lumpy, the fondant was bald in places, and Sienna must have used up Harper's entire store of pre-made marzipan flowers on the top.

It belonged on a Pinterest fail.

"Things not going so hot?" Sienna asked.

Harper laughed. "Was it that obvious?"

"You looked like someone ran over Mister Mittens." Sienna's eyes flicked to the cameras. Thankfully, they were focused on Harry—who still was having a hard time with the frosting after rejecting Harper's multiple attempts to help him. "You want to talk about it?"

Harper shook her head.

"Is it that production assistant you spent yesterday with?"

Harper's eyes went wide, and Sienna nudged her. "Stay cool. I don't think the chase thing will work twice. But tell me about it later?"

Harper knew it would do her some good to talk through everything that had happened over the past few days. And she owed it to her sister. Sienna had put herself out there and made herself look ridiculous for the cameras all to cover for Harper and Audrey.

But Audrey was the one Harper wanted. The one she needed. And if she was really being honest with herself, it was Milo too. The big brother that should have been there to intimidate Harper's boyfriends—if she'd had any—and tell her to not take any crap from boys who had been gone for so long. Audrey disappearing just highlighted how much Harper still needed her older siblings. She was used to handling other people's messes, but she needed at least some backup when it came to her own mess of a life.

Now that she'd seen Austin for who he really was, she needed her family more than ever. But could she admit everything to perfect, dazzling Sienna? Could she trust her with years of heartache?

"Harper?" Sienna looked at her sister expectantly.

Harper shook her head. "I'll be fine."

4 Days Until Dream Wedding

WAS Harper trying to give Austin a heart attack? He'd asked for interesting, not a frosting fight.

And now everyone was just silently decorating their cakes, while Harper walked around and quietly pointed out things they could improve. Austin's brilliant plan was turning into a bigger flop as each second ticked away on his watch. But it was too late now to pull the plug.

At least Jennifer seemed to be happy. Austin found little comfort, however, in knowing that the more secret looks he gave her, the safer Harper was. This added competition would do great things for the Flour Girl Bakery. If it got on the air, that is.

"Do you think we should see if the bride feels up to coming down to help judge?" Jennifer asked halfway through the allotted hour of decorating time. She had a hand on his shoulder, and it took everything in him to not shrug it off. Instead, he placed his hand on top of hers for a brief moment.

"Let her rest. If she's been up sick all night and then all day, she'll want some sleep."

"I think it's cute that you still think she's sick and not faking it." She paused and then her mouth fell open. "Unless you know what's going on."

Austin shook his head, the movement a little too jerky. "I don't know what you're talking about. Everyone says Audrey is sick."

Jennifer reached out and grabbed his hand. "I meant it when I said I'd keep all your secrets. And it's easier for me to do that if I know what you're hiding."

"I'm not hiding anything," he said, taking his hand back. He was worried that Bruce would notice the extra attention between him and Jennifer.

When Austin looked over to where the producer stood, however, Bruce wasn't even paying attention to what was happening in the kitchen. He had his ear to his phone and was whispering with his mouth covered. Austin's stomach twisted into the familiar knot it had been in all day.

"What's up with Bruce?" he asked Jennifer, who just shrugged.

Austin looked at his watch to check how much time they had left. With a pang of remembering all of Harper's teasing about it, he signaled to her that there were fifteen minutes left, just as Jason Castle announced the same thing. He was met with her stormy glare, and she whirled on her feet to turn away from him.

He deserved it, he knew, for being so cold to her. But what choice did he have?

"I heard this competition was your idea."

Austin looked up from his clipboard to see Jason Castle standing in front of him with his perma-smile of blindingly white teeth.

Austin nodded. "Yeah."

"That's great. Really great." Jason reached out and put his hand on Austin's shoulder.

The contact made him shudder. Austin was so tired of people laying their hands on him all the time. Meanwhile, the one person he wanted to touch and kiss was angry at him and would probably never speak to him again.

He shrugged out of Jason's touch. "Thanks."

"I'm serious. This business isn't for the faint of heart. You need to be fluid and able to adapt or you end up like Kip Kippler."

Austin's brows furrowed. "Who?"

Jason laughed like they were sharing an inside joke. "Exactly. Kip used to be the host of one of the most popular game shows. But he got stuck in his ways. His show got cancelled, and nobody knows who he is anymore."

Kinda like Jason Castles, Austin thought to himself.

"Which is why I'm glad to see you stepping up," Jason continued. "This family has been an absolute nightmare, and you're saving all of our butts whether you know it or not."

Austin didn't like Jason, or really anyone else on the set right now, but he still felt a small swell of pride at Jason's words. The host might be washed up, but he knew what he was talking about.

Austin was on the cusp of everything he'd always wanted.

Well, almost everything. He might get to keep his job and have his pick of projects thanks to Bruce's reference. And, if Jason were to be believed, he was doing a good job despite the many distractions. But what was the point of seeing his career dreams come true if he didn't get Harper in the end?

He stood there in silence while Jason continued to drone on about the differences between Hollywood ten years ago and now, barely registering any of his words. Who knew how long it would have gone on, if Bruce didn't come charging into the middle of the kitchen, finally off his phone call.

"Okay, folks. I think it's time to wrap this competition up. You've got five more minutes."

A chorus of groans went through the room.

"But I haven't finished putting all the flowers on," Sienna said.

"I'm sure you can figure something out," Bruce answered, his voice calm—but not in the scary way that Bruce usually spoke.

It was almost reassuring, meant to put Sienna at ease. But the casual remark had the opposite effect on Austin. His already anxious mind went on high alert. Something was going on.

"But what if I can't?" Sienna asked.

Austin rubbed his hand over his face. Harper's sister was unbelievable. Couldn't she pick up on the tension in the room? He wanted to shush her, not caring what Bruce or anyone else would think, but was thankful when Fox walked over and did it instead.

"Everyone's cakes will be just fine. It's not like they're the actual cakes for the wedding," Bruce said. "Let's get these cakes to the front of the shop. I'm ready to get the judging underway."

Austin knew there was something going on. But what was it?

He watched as Bruce walked over to Jason and gave him some small index cards. The two men talked in hushed voices as the cameramen readjusted their positions around the room, and the wedding party scrambled to put finishing touches on their individual cakes.

The five minutes went by faster than Austin wanted, and soon everyone was crowded in the front seating area of the bakery. It was a small space and even though they'd removed all of Harper's carefully arranged chairs and tables, there was barely room to breathe. Austin stood off to the side, just out of the view of the cameras, as Jason started talking to the group.

"Alright, alright. You've all been given the opportunity to show what you're made of in the kitchen. Some of you made it further than others." He paused and looked at Harry, who had an angry scowl on his face.

"And others got a little creative." This time Jason's gaze went to Wade. The heavily tattooed groomsman laughed it off and beamed proudly at his cake. It had an uneven layer of frosting and random shapes etched into the buttercream. At least none of them resembled the sculpture Austin had caught him making earlier.

Jason turned to the groom-to-be. "So, Eli, which do you think your lovely bride will enjoy the most as the groom's cake?"

Eli was pale and trembling, a physical representation of how everyone felt. Audrey was missing—or sick, depending on who you talked to. Any mention of her name set Austin's heart racing, so he could only imagine what Eli must be feeling right now. The groom-to-be wiped a trickle of sweat off his forehead. "I, uh…"

"I think I can answer that myself."

All heads turned toward the sound of the loud, female voice that came from the door of the bakery.

Audrey was back.

TWENTY

4 Days Until Dream Wedding

HARPER'S STOMACH PLUMMETED. She'd be right there on the floor beside it if she hadn't been leaning against the display case as she waited for the cake judging.

The room was silent for what felt like an eternity as everyone gaped at Audrey's sudden appearance. Harper struggled to find her voice, but it never came.

Thankfully, Sienna recovered first and ran over to their oldest sister.

"I'm so glad you're feeling better!"

All cameras focused on the two of them, which left everyone else to work through their shock in relative privacy. Reagan came over to Harper, who was still gripping onto the display case for dear life.

"Jason doesn't look that surprised."

Harper's gaze went to the host, who looked perfectly unaffected, and then to the rest of the crew. Bruce, Jennifer, Austin. Each one of them was focused on Audrey, but not even a hint of shock was on their faces. "You're right. There's a reason we're the only ones who are surprised."

Reagan's eyes went wide. "Do you think they all knew? Do you think this was part of the show?"

Harper wanted to throw up, but instead she nodded. "It has to be. Unless they all really believed she was sick this whole time."

"Despite what Sienna said, I know I'm not that good an actor," Fox said, appearing behind the girls. "I don't think I was fooling anyone." He had his arms folded across his chest and was gazing at Bruce like he wanted to strangle him.

Harper had someone else in her own murderous sights. With a laser focus that she was surprised didn't burn through his skin, she caught Austin's eye and jerked her head toward the kitchen. Not waiting to see if he got the message, she turned on her heel and barreled through the double doors.

It was a mess. Tiffany looked up, relieved, from where she was cleaning up the mounds of sprinkles and frosting and tiny bits of cut fondant. Harper had originally planned to stay and help her clean everything up.

That was, before her sister popped up out of nowhere like it wasn't a big deal for her to be missing for days at a time without telling anyone.

Now Harper wasn't sure what she was going to do.

"Audrey's here," she said.

Tiffany stopped wiping the counter and looked up, her eyes wide. "She is?"

Harper nodded. "I don't think I can stay and clean."

"That's fine. I'm sure I can handle it myself."

Harper gave her a grateful smile. Tiffany worked so hard. But that gratitude only lasted until Austin came walking through the kitchen door. Glancing over her shoulder and seeing his stupid, handsome face annoyed her more than the endless requests from local "influencers" for free cakes in exchange for exposure.

"Office," she growled at Austin before stalking off to the tiny broom closet she used for making calls and filing invoices.

With the door closed, Harper realized what a bad idea this had been.

Most of the space was taken up with the computer desk and filing cabinet she'd shoved in there the first week of opening the shop when her mother had asked where she planned on putting her office. Stacks of papers sat on top of recipe books, and half the drawers on the filing cabinet were open. It felt entirely too small with them both inside.

She stuck a finger in his chest. "You knew about Audrey coming back today."

"What? Of course not."

"Then why don't you look surprised?"

He threw his hands in the air, knocking a pile of papers off a shelf on the wall. The twitch in his arm told Harper he was dying to pick it up. "It's my job to deal with the unexpected."

"I'm supposed to believe that? After everything you've done to me?"

The tiny bit of hope she'd been holding onto shattered when Austin didn't even try to deny it.

"Look, I'm sorry about earlier. I didn't mean it."

As much as she wanted Austin to be honest with her, it was hard to hear him flat out say he didn't mean anything he'd said during their time together.

Harper bit her trembling lip. "I know that. I would have agreed to help you just for Audrey's sake. You didn't have to make me think—" She took a deep breath. "You didn't have to lie about caring for me all this time. Pretend to want me to come visit."

"But I do want—" He reached out to take her hand, but bumped into the swinging lamp on the desk. It spun on its base to whack Harper in the arm.

"Ow!"

"Well you really should clean in here." He sucked in a breath and ran his hands through his hair. More errant papers fluttered to the floor. "That's not what I—"

"Just go." Harper's voice shook, but she wouldn't give him the satisfaction of crying, just so he and Jennifer could laugh about it later. Stupid Harper, thinking she was good enough for someone like Austin.

"I didn't know about Audrey. But I'll find out what I can and let you know."

"Don't bother," she said and stormed out of the office. Without a backward glance, she tore through the back door of the bakery and out into the cool summer night.

———

IF IT WASN'T for the stupid contract she'd signed, Harper would be gone by now.

Actually, after everything that happened with Audrey and Austin, Harper wasn't sure even the contract was enough to keep her at The Emerald Inn.

Her apartment was so close.

The idea of going home and curling up on the couch in her PJs with Mister Mittens purring in her lap was more appealing by the minute.

Harper eyed her suitcase in the corner of the hotel

room. It would take her five minutes to pack up all of her things, and within fifteen she could be back in town and watching *The Office* if no one spotted her.

She silently weighed her options, but when her mind conjured up the image of Austin and Jennifer getting cozy in *her* bakery, she decided she'd had enough. Harper would come back to watch Audrey and Eli exchange vows, but until then, she was going home.

She started grabbing her dirty clothes from the corner of the room that she'd designated as the makeshift hamper and haphazardly shoved all of it into her suitcase. A smug satisfaction rolled through at the thought of Austin cringing to see such a messy packing job. She could practically hear him droning on about the proper technique to avoid wrinkles. She should be thanking Jennifer for saving her from the affection of a controlling liar.

Next were her toiletries. Each little bottle of face wash and lotion was a reminder that nothing she could do would ever make her as pretty as her sisters or Tiffany or Jennifer. Harper had just finished putting her useless makeup into her case and was zipping it up when a knock came at the door.

She stilled and held her breath.

The knock came again. "Come on, Harper. I know you're in there."

Sienna. One of the very few people Harper was not mad at right now. But she still didn't want to talk about what was going on with her. If Harper started explaining what had happened over the last few days, Sienna would only try to convince her to stay.

And Sienna could be very persuading.

No, it would be better to stay quiet for a few

minutes until her younger sister left. Then Harper could finish packing and sneak away before anyone noticed. Audrey had managed it, so it must not be that hard.

The knocking continued. "I can do this all night," said Sienna from the other side of the door. "Eventually you're going to break."

Harper pressed her lips together. Sienna wanted to get into a battle of wills right now? Little did she know that Harper was still fired up enough that she wasn't going to be the first to give in. She had years of frustration built up and was pretty sure her battered heart could ignore a red-wagon-full-of-puppies level of persuasion if she had to.

Under the cover of Sienna's increasingly loud and insistent banging, Harper finished packing her things and set them near the door. Everything was ready for the perfect getaway, just as soon as her sister had given up.

Harper sat on the bed to wait it out, and Sienna got creative with her knocking. She was tapping out different rhythms and started singing along. She did pop songs, rap songs, and even the *Barney* theme song—which just about made Harper give in.

But she stayed firm in her resolution and didn't open the door.

After forty minutes of singing, the knocking stopped. "Fine. Be like that. But I'm not the one you're mad at, and it's not fair to take it out on me. I even brought brownies and everything."

The pain in Sienna's voice ripped through Harper. She really wasn't being fair. Harper took a deep breath, got off the bed, and opened the door. On the other side stood Sienna, and she looked as tired and confused as Harper felt.

Her hair was pulled back in a messy ponytail and there were black smudges of mascara under her eyes. Her shoulders relaxed when she saw Harper. "About time."

Harper lifted her mouth into a sad smile as she stood aside to let Sienna in. "Next time, try leading with the brownies."

Sienna snorted and held out the brown paper Flour Girl carryout bag. "I'll try to remember that next time."

Harper took the bag and waved her inside the room. "Hopefully, there isn't a next time."

Her sister plopped onto the bed and considered this for a moment. "Where did you go earlier? None of us saw you leave." Then her eyes spotted the suitcases by the door. "And where exactly do you think you're going?"

Harper shrugged.

Sienna jumped up from the bed. "Seriously? After what Audrey put us through, you were going to do the same thing? Did you ever stop to consider what that would do to everyone? What that would do to *me*?"

No. Harper hadn't. A wave of shame crashed over her. "I'm sorry. I'm just so confused. I don't know what to do."

"You and me both, sis."

"Did Audrey explain why she left?"

Sienna shook her head. "No. Bruce welcomed her back. And then she judged the cakes like she hadn't been missing for almost two days."

Harper started pacing back and forth in the small room.

"Well, it's obviously some kind of scheme. And everyone seems to be in on it besides me and you." Harper paused to think. "And Fox."

"Really?" Sienna looked doubtful. "You think everyone else knew except the three of us. Even Mom?"

Harper shrugged. Anyone was fair game at this point. But then, she got a great idea. She looked at Sienna with a bright smile. "Come with me."

"What?"

"I planned to hide out at my house for the next few days. If Audrey and Eli get married, I plan to come back. But until then we can——"

"Are you crazy?"

Harper was stunned into silence.

"*If* they get married? Are you even hearing yourself right now? I don't know what's going on with you, but you're not leaving." Sienna put her hands on her hips. "It's only four days until the wedding. Three, really, since today's almost over. I know you're upset, and trust me, I'm really angry too. But we are not going to mess this up for Audrey, because one day we won't feel like this, and if we do anything to jeopardize her big day, we're going to feel horrible. Forever."

Wow. The mini tirade sounded nothing like the Sienna she knew.

When had her baby sister become such a grownup? Audrey and Harper liked to tease her about her big, glamorous New York City life, but Sienna had just as much determination as her older sisters. The Hudson women did not give up easily. If Harper left now, she'd be no better than the Hudson men. Or Austin.

Harper nodded. "Okay. I won't leave, and I won't do

anything impulsive. But I still want to know what's going on."

"Me too."

"Then maybe you'll give me a chance to explain?" Audrey's timid voice caused both girls' heads to snap toward the door.

Their oldest sister lifted a corner of her mouth. "You left the door unlocked. Hope it's okay that I let myself in."

4 Days Until Dream Wedding

HARPER FELT her stomach plummet for the second time that night. She and Audrey had become so close these last couple of years. At least, she thought they had. Now it felt like she didn't know the woman standing in front of her at all. With a thump, she sat down on the bed, Sienna right beside her.

"I'm sorry I disappeared." Audrey shifted on her feet by the closed door.

"Are you?" Harper muttered under her breath, promptly earning an elbow in her ribs and a stern look from Sienna.

"Of course I am." Audrey reached out her hands but dropped them at her sisters' stormy faces. "But Bruce made me promise not to say anything. He came to me with a production assistant after the karaoke contest and told me I needed to go away for a couple of days."

"And so you just went?" Harper folded her arms and glared at Audrey. Sienna might have made some excellent points about regretting their actions later if they did anything to mess up the wedding, but Audrey was acting like nothing had happened. Harper felt like a pot about to boil over.

"He told me we needed to build up more drama. He wanted to see what you two would do."

"So you just left while we were freaking out, trying to cover for what we assumed was our runaway bride sister. I hope you and Mom enjoyed your spa day?"

Audrey shook her head. "No, it wasn't like that. Nobody else knew. And Bruce had a very good reason for me leaving."

"Yeah, the drama." Sienna rolled her eyes. "Which if he doesn't get, you don't get your wedding."

Audrey bit her lip. "There's that. But there's another reason he had me leave."

Harper lifted her brows waiting for the explanation that never came.

"I'm sorry. I can't tell you. But I promise it's a good thing." She paused. "Or at least I think it is."

Harper ran a hand over her face. "I'm getting really tired of this. Everyone has secrets, and I don't know who I can trust anymore."

Audrey sat down next to her on the bed and wrapped her arm over her shoulders. "What do you mean?"

"Bruce, you, Austin."

Audrey jerked back. "Who's Austin?"

"He's a production assistant that Harper is supposed to be flirting with," Sienna explained. "Though I don't know why she thinks she can trust him. He works for Bruce."

Harper ignored Sienna and kept her eyes trained on

Audrey. "You know, he's the guy who went to you with Bruce after the karaoke contest."

Audrey's brows lowered. "It wasn't a guy. It was a girl with dark hair."

Huh. So maybe Austin hadn't known about Audrey after all. But he was still part of the crew, and his job depended on abiding by the rules of whatever mind games Bruce wanted to play.

"But I want to know more about why you were flirting with this Austin guy." Audrey gave Harper a sly smile that made her irritation flare.

"That's none of your—"

"Because she was trying to cover for your disappearance," Sienna said, crossing her arms.

Audrey's face fell. "And I'm really sorry about that. I wanted to tell you guys, but Bruce made me promise not to. Not if we wanted the second part of the surprise."

"You mean the thing you can't tell us," Harper grumbled.

"I'm sorry."

"You keep saying that," Sienna said.

Audrey threw up her hands. "Because I don't know what else to say. You're obviously mad at me. I get that. But I can't change anything now." She paused. "I don't know that I would even if I could at this point."

"Is that supposed to be reassuring?" Harper glared at her. The more Audrey talked, the more upset Harper got. "You disappeared for two days and were more than willing to keep secrets from your sisters and best friend just to get your dream wedding. The same people who had put their lives on hold for two weeks, who were worried sick and covered for you."

Audrey was almost as good at lying as Austin was.

His earlier performance had been awfully convincing. Maybe he hadn't known about Audrey, but he'd been following Bruce's orders from day one. He had Harper believing he was putting his job on the line to help her, and like a fool, she'd fallen for it. Of course he wouldn't risk his big break for the girl he'd left behind without a second glance at graduation.

He'd taken advantage of Harper's feelings to get the footage they'd needed for the big dramatic reveal.

And now that things were all out in the open, he was free to go back to Jennifer, the gorgeous girl he'd obviously wanted all along.

It was all too much, and Harper started crying. She hadn't meant to, and definitely didn't want to show how affected she was in front of Audrey while she was still mad at her. But her tear ducts didn't listen to logic, and within seconds, she was sobbing loud and hard.

"Oh, sweetie." Audrey wrapped her arms around Harper.

She shook her off, the tears still falling, and looked at Sienna instead. "I'm in love with Austin."

Sienna's eyes went wide a split second before she started laughing.

Audrey smacked her. "Stop. She's obviously upset about it."

"What?" Sienna covered her giggling mouth with a hand. "Reagan and I asked her to flirt with him to try to get information about *Wedding Games* while you were missing. She's obviously overwhelmed because she can't be in love with him after one night in Eli's cabin."

Audrey's face whipped toward Harper. "You took one of the crew members to Eli's cabin?"

"Calm down," Sienna said. "They were looking for you."

"And Harper thought she should take a total stranger to the middle of nowhere?"

"He was helping her!"

"Or maybe Austin was trying to help Bruce get his drama-filled show. He went out there to trick Harper into thinking she had feelings for him after one day."

The two sisters were standing now, yelling into each other's faces, and Harper didn't want to know how much things would escalate if she didn't interrupt. Her tears dried up, she stood up from her spot on the bed and sniffed. "I've known him since college."

Sienna and Audrey immediately stopped yelling at each other, turned to Harper, and screeched "what?" in unison.

"We met freshman year. We lived across the hall from each other and became best friends almost immediately."

"Best friends?" Sienna asked. Her eyes narrowed, not in suspicion, but more like she was trying to process the information. "You never mentioned him."

"You were still in high school dealing with your popular girl life, and Audrey was busy with her first year of teaching. It wasn't important." Or, at least, that's what Harper had told herself as she'd slowly but surely fallen in love with Austin. And since there had been no chance of him ever loving her back, why bother her sisters with her dorm room drama?

"So, you've known Austin for eight years?" Audrey asked.

Harper nodded.

"Which meant you knew he was going to be here."

Audrey shook her head and huffed. "And you're mad that I kept secrets?"

"I didn't know he would be here."

"But you just said you were best friends," Sienna said.

Harper closed her eyes, not wanting to see her sisters' reaction. She already felt utterly humiliated to realize that Austin had been playing her the entire time. She couldn't bear to see the disappointment on Audrey or Sienna's face. Or worse—their pity. "We *were* best friends until I told him that I was in love with him...and he walked away. I haven't seen him or talked to him in four years. Seeing him the first day of filming was a kick in the gut."

The mood of the room shifted, and Harper could literally feel when Audrey's accusations dissipated. With them went Harper's anger at her older sister. This show was making them crazy, and it was foolish to fight with each other when there were other people messing with their lives way more.

"It's why you were so distracted when Bruce interviewed us," Sienna said. "And so absent-minded about everything."

Harper shrugged "I thought I would work through it in a day or two on my own."

"I wish we'd known," Audrey said. "We could have listened while you gushed about him."

"Not that it would do any good." Harper sniffed as the tears finally started to dry. "He doesn't feel the same way."

"Are you sure?" Sienna asked. "Not even after a romantic night stranded together in the cabin?"

Harper's cheeks heated.

"Oh my goodness." Sienna's eyes went wide. "What happened in the cabin?"

Harper covered her face in her hands. "We may have kissed."

"And yet you don't think he feels anything for you?" Sienna asked.

Harper dropped her hands at her sides with a resigned sigh. "I don't know. I thought he did. But now I think it was just a ruse to keep me distracted and to get me to do whatever the show needed. Using my bakery. Getting good footage of me running around the inn all panicked."

"Maybe..." Audrey rubbed her chin. "But I swear he didn't know. It was only Bruce, the female production assistant, Eli, and me. He said we had to keep it a secret."

Harper rolled her eyes. "Oh yeah. Because Bruce is so trustworthy."

"I'm serious. We signed a contract."

"Another one?" Sienna sighed loudly. "I tried to tell you that this whole thing was a mistake."

"Can we not get into that right now?" Audrey whined. "We've got other things going on."

Like the endless secrets between crew and contestants, and even family members. Harper didn't like being suspicious of her own sisters. But she still wasn't sure if she could trust anyone. Especially not Austin. If Audrey was right, and Austin wasn't the person who snuck Audrey off The Emerald Inn property, then...

Harper sat up. "What was the name of the production assistant?"

Audrey's face crinkled up. "Jessica...? Wait, no. Jennifer. Her name was Jennifer."

Harper let out a weak laugh. "Well, that explains how Austin knows. The two of them are an item, and I'm sure she told him so he could distract us. I feel like such an idiot."

"What a jerk," Sienna said. "I know this isn't going to be easy to hear, but maybe it's for the best. Can you imagine if you had started dating?"

An image of her and Austin curled up together on the couch laughing filled her mind. What would it have been like if he'd turned around and kissed her on graduation day? Would they be married by now? Even with his betrayal, it was hard not to want that. She felt like the biggest sucker in the world.

"You know what?" Audrey stood up, her eyes blazing. "Screw the contracts and the secrets. I don't care about the wedding anymore. I don't care about the secrets. This show is tearing our family apart, and I'm going to fix everything."

Audrey ignored Sienna and Harper's protests as she stormed out the door. She was in scary teacher mode, and her younger sisters exchanged wary glances at her intensity. Whatever she was going to do wasn't good.

Sienna bit her bottom lip. "I think I'm going to check in on Reagan and see how she's doing. Audrey's disappearance was hard on all of us, and she's been out of the loop for a lot of major revelations." Her eyes went to the suitcase that was still in the corner of the room. "Do I need to worry about you running away if I leave?"

Harper shook her head. "I promise I won't leave."

"Good." Sienna leaned in and kissed her cheek. "I love you. I'm sorry that this Austin guy is such a jerk. You're gorgeous and amazing. And until you find a guy who can appreciate you, and won't lie to you, don't settle."

Harper's chest tightened at the compliment. Sienna had never called her gorgeous before. "Thanks."

"I'll check in on you later, but I don't know when. I'll need to make sure there are no cameras around."

Harper nodded. "I know."

With one last hug, Sienna was out the door, leaving Harper alone in the room. She felt better now that everything was off her chest. If nothing else good came from this stupid show, at least her relationship with her sisters was back on track.

Despite all of that, she knew it could never totally fill the hole that Austin had left in her heart.

TWENTY-TWO

4 Days Until Dream Wedding

"THAT COULDN'T HAVE GONE BETTER if I had planned it," Bruce said to the production team once they were back at The Emerald Inn. His remark was met with laughter, but Austin wanted to throw up.

He *had* planned it. Bruce had known the entire time where Audrey had been, and now Harper thought Austin was in on it. When he'd tried to explain the truth of the situation to her, everything had come out wrong.

He'd spent the last hour overanalyzing his every word and hating himself for losing his temper in her messy office. As difficult as being in a cluttered workspace was for him, it was a nice reminder that the Harper he knew and loved hadn't completely disappeared. She was a successful business owner with her life together, but still let papers pile up. He loved that about her. Instead of saying that, however, he'd snapped at her and ruined everything. The shock of Audrey's return combined with the smug smiles on some of the production crew's faces had put him on edge right before he'd followed her into the kitchen.

Austin shook himself out of his thoughts when Bruce started diving into instructions for the next few hours. "We still need to get interviews with everyone asking them what they think about Audrey's return." Bruce looked at his watch. "And we need to do it fast before they have a chance to calm down. I want a camera on her sister, Harper, ASAP. She looked like she'd had the rug pulled out from her. And why wouldn't she after trying to cover for Audrey for two days."

Another wave of laughter went through the crowd. They were all laughing at Harper. They found her pain entertaining, but they hadn't seen the way she'd made herself sick over finding Audrey.

Austin swallowed the unease brewing in his stomach. Reality television had always been something far removed from him. Just a bunch a nameless faces who were dumb enough to sign up for their own humiliation. Working on different sets over the years and seeing the things producers put these people through, it was no wonder the stars of some reality shows lost it. The game was rigged, and the house always won—or in this case, Bruce always won.

Only now it was much more personal.

Jennifer appeared next to Austin and linked her arm in his. "Hey," she whispered and pulled him close. But Austin was too focused on Bruce, so preoccupied by everything the producer was saying that he didn't even push Jennifer away.

"Watch out for Sienna," Bruce said. "She thinks she's a professional actress and will pretend like she didn't know anything was wrong. But if you push her buttons—maybe mention her missing brother, Milo— she gets emotional and makes mistakes."

Jennifer nudged Austin with her shoulder. "Ain't that the truth."

"Eli was in on Audrey's disappearance, so we don't need to get footage of him. I already had someone get his interview."

Silently, Austin wondered who else knew. His eyes scanned the crowd looking for some kind of tell from his co-workers, but everyone's eyes stayed glued to the front of the room.

"I also want to make sure we sit down with the groomsmen. Fox was suspiciously absent yesterday, and I have a feeling he was in cahoots with the girls. Harry is always good for some footage. Whoever interviews him, make sure to bring up the cake. He looked like he was having a hard time with it. And Wade, he's going to be the guy the ladies fall for. Make him look good because I may have plans for him."

"I'd like to have some plans with him," a woman in the back said. She and a few others giggled.

Jennifer squeezed Austin's arm. "Don't worry, I only want you."

He was not at all worried. In fact, he would prefer if Jennifer wanted Wade instead of him.

"Austin, Jennifer. I want you two on interviews. Grab some equipment and a cameraman, and get moving," Bruce said before he barked out orders to the rest of the crew.

Austin didn't wait to see who got assigned where and practically ran out of the room. He was already creating a mental list of things he needed to grab from the tent outside before he could get started. And he wanted to get started immediately. This was his chance to talk to Harper again. Maybe it wasn't too late for him to explain what had happened. True, she'd been pretty angry the last time he'd seen her. Hopefully she'd cooled down. It wasn't like she could deny an interview with him. It was in the contract. He'd simply claim the girls before Jennifer got a chance. He opened his mouth—

"I'll get the bridesmaids, you get the groomsmen," Jennifer said, appearing next to him just as he entered the tent.

Austin's breath caught. "Oh. I kinda thought I could get the bridesmaids, and *you* could get the groomsmen."

She stopped and looked at him, her face stern. "So you can talk to Harper?"

Austin gave a jerky shake of his head and uneasy laugh. He started piling supplies into a backpack. "Why would you think that?"

She rolled her eyes. "Do me a favor and stop treating me like I'm some clueless LA bimbo. I'm good at what I do, and after *Wedding Games,* I'm going to have a lot more opportunities."

Austin had been counting on the same being true for him, especially after his cake decorating contest idea. He just had to keep it together for a few more days, and he'd be that much closer to the career of his dreams. But the pull toward Harper couldn't be ignored. "I want to interview the bridesmaids because I want to make sure Harper's okay after what happened with her sister."

Jennifer grabbed Austin's bag and shook her head. "What is it about that girl? The wedding is in four days, and after that, you'll be back in LA where you belong. Why do you care so much?" She swung the bag onto her back, and they walked back outside and headed toward the inn.

Austin almost said "because I love her" but he bit his

tongue. Jennifer would find a way to use those feelings against him.

He shrugged, hoping it looked casual. "Because even if I never see her again, that was a cheap shot, and you know it."

"It's reality TV, Austin. They know what they're getting into."

"That doesn't make it right."

They'd just stepped back inside the inn. Jennifer looked up and down the hall before she pulled Austin into a closet. It wasn't the makeshift safe room, and there was a giant mop bucket in the room that took up a lot of space. The two of them were closer than was entirely comfortable for Austin.

She spoke in hushed, hurried words, her eyes fixed on his. "I'm only telling you this because I'm serious about us dating when we get back to LA. And I hope that when I tell you, you'll know that you can trust me with your secrets too."

Austin nodded, his heart pounding. "Okay." This was either going to be really good or really bad.

"I knew Audrey didn't run away."

Really bad, then.

"What?" Austin's voice boomed in the small room.

"Shh." Jennifer's eyes went wide. "Do you want to get caught?"

Caught in a small closet with Jennifer while he still hadn't made amends with Harper? Not even a little. He shook his head.

"Look, I shouldn't have even told you this."

"No, you should have told me sooner."

"*No*, because Bruce and I knew you would help Harper if you thought there was a problem."

Was he that transparent?

"I needed you to tell me what was going on."

All this time she'd had ulterior motives. And then she thought Austin would still want to date her after this? Yeah right. It was the final straw.

"Why would you do that to her sisters? Do you even feel remorse for stressing them out?"

She laughed. "Of course I don't. I did it because Bruce said if I helped him, he would give me a spot on his next project. It's supposed to be really great too. Better than *Wedding Games*."

She rattled on and on about how Bruce had caught her during the karaoke competition and asked if she wanted to be part of a special project.

But Austin struggled to pay attention. His jumbled thoughts fought to understand what Jennifer was saying. It was one thing to manipulate the contestants on the show, which was to be expected. But to pit crew members against each other? Austin was just now realizing the extent of Bruce's mind games.

Was this what they meant when they talked about show business eating people alive?

"I'm done," he said, interrupting Jennifer's one-sided conversation.

"What?"

"I'm not cut out for this job. Thank you for helping me realize that." He opened the door and started walking down the hall toward the last place he'd seen Bruce. He needed to tell him now before he lost his nerve.

Jennifer was right behind him. "Don't do this," she pleaded. "Think about how hard you've worked to stay on Bruce's good side. Your cake decorating contest idea was really good."

"Yeah, but he's already singled you out as his pick for who to work with next, hasn't he? So it doesn't matter." A few days ago, he would have been unbearably jealous of Jennifer. Not anymore.

"If you quit before the show's done filming, he'll make sure you never get another job in television."

"I'm counting on it." Austin smiled to himself. While he should have felt nervous or anxious about ruining everything he'd worked so hard for over the years, he felt a tremendous peace about his spur of the moment decision.

He was at the door to the meeting room where he could hear Bruce's cold, hard voice shouting out instructions. Two deep breaths, and he stepped forward to open the door, but then it opened and Jason Castle walked out.

"Oh, thank goodness." Jennifer sighed. "Can you please talk some sense into Austin?"

Jason's brows lowered. "Uh, sure." He glanced at Austin, who just shrugged. He didn't have time for this. He had to get this over with so he could find Harper as soon as possible.

But Jennifer was right behind him, blocking him in. "Austin wants to leave the show."

"Why?" Jason folded his arms and tilted his head.

Jennifer snorted. "Because he's cracking under the pressure. Can you explain that it's normal to feel overwhelmed, and help me convince him not to make Bruce angry?"

Jason shook his head. "Do not make that guy angry.

He's got connections, he's friends with all the bigwigs. It will be near impossible to get work again."

Austin tried not to roll his eyes. They were acting like Bruce was king of the universe. "Would that be so bad?"

"That depends." Jason chuckled. "If you're content living in some Podunk town like Wellspring for the rest of your life, then go for it. But you've got to remember, following your dreams is about sacrifices. Do you think I got where I am today without making tough choices?"

"Of course not," Jennifer said, her eyes glued to Jason.

"Thanks for the advice. I need to talk to Bruce." Austin tried to push past him, but he stayed put in front of the closed door.

Jason looked him up and down. "Kid, how old are you?"

"Why?"

"Because you don't look old enough to know what you really want out of life yet. You'll learn with time that a window doesn't always open when you close a door. Sometimes you have to bang on windows all over town before one opens a tiny crack."

Austin looked at Jason, for the first time seeing just how caked on his makeup was. Instead of hiding the lines on his face, it made each one into a deep valley full of past sorrows. Jason had been in this business since before Austin was born. How much had he given up to do what he loved?

"Would you have done anything differently?" Austin asked him.

"Like I said, it's all about making sacrifices. If I had realized that sooner, I wouldn't be stuck here doing a show like this, that's for sure. You gotta know what you're willing to give up to get where you want to be."

The thing was, Austin already knew what he was willing to give up to follow his dreams. He marched inside the meeting room without a second thought, and quit.

TWENTY-THREE

4 Days Until Dream Wedding

AUSTIN PACKED his suitcase in record time, but when the time came to talk to Harper, his feet suddenly felt like lead. The last time he'd seen her, they'd fought. Before that, he'd been rude and flirting with Jennifer.

Not exactly ideal behavior to win her favor.

He hadn't thought about that when Bruce yelled at him, the vein on his forehead throbbing. He'd been so excited to quit his job and pursue Harper, that he hadn't stopped to think about how it would go.

And now he was second guessing whether or not he should tell Harper, or leave again—and never come back.

This was why he always had a plan. The uncertainty about his next step was eating him alive from the inside. A creeping unease made its way up his body and into his stomach, threatening to overflow in a spectacular display of digestive pyrotechnics.

He needed air. He grabbed his suitcase and headed to the front desk to stash it while he took a walk around the property to clear his head. The crew had shared cars from the airport, so he'd need to call a cab eventually. But first, a walk.

It was dark, and the property was quiet. His shoulders instantly relaxed when the fresh mountain breeze hit his face. It was easier to think now that he was outside and away from the buzz of voices in the inn. He made his way toward the barn at the back of the property, thankful for the lights scattered throughout the trail to illuminate the way. It would be empty since it was night and being alone was the best way to sort through his thoughts.

"Hey!"

The voice was far behind him, but Austin kept walking. It wasn't Harper, and now that he'd quit, there was no one else he needed to listen to.

"Hey!"

He kept walking but finally stopped when a hand pulled on his arm.

"I don't know what my sister ever saw in a jerk like you."

Austin whirled around to see Audrey standing with her hands on her hips, glaring at him like he'd just kicked a litter of puppies.

"Excuse me?" He knew he should try to win some points with Harper's sister, but she'd just interrupted his vital planning meeting with himself. He didn't have time for this.

"You have a lot of nerve, coming here, messing with Harper." Audrey's eyes blazed, and Austin took a step back. Apparently all the Hudson sisters were impressively scary when irritated.

"What have I done to mess with her? All I've been doing is trying to help her."

Audrey held up a finger to her chin like she was thinking hard. "Oh, I don't know, maybe how you tricked her into liking you again just so you could use her bakery and do whatever else Bruce told you to do."

"That seems like a very elaborate scheme for someone who didn't even know she'd be here."

Audrey rolled her eyes. "Yeah, okay."

"Really, I didn't know she'd be here." He ran a hand across his face. "I didn't know you'd go missing. I don't know anything right now."

She snorted. "No kidding."

"I do know I hurt her by pretending to be with Jennifer."

Audrey's eyes narrowed. "Pretending?"

Austin looked off into the trees, embarrassed to be admitting so much to someone he barely knew. "Jennifer threatened to tell Bruce that I knew Harper from college unless I was her boyfriend. I thought if I could make Jennifer think I liked her, she'd back off from Harper."

"Well that's...devious."

Austin barked out a laugh. "I thought she was my friend, that we'd help each other out, but she just went off the deep end on this job. She knew the whole time where you were. Meanwhile, I was in a panic running around with Harper looking for you."

Audrey winced. "I really didn't like lying to Harper."

"Neither did I, but it was to protect her. To protect your family."

Audrey frowned. "You don't know us."

He shrugged. "I'd like to. If she'd give me the chance."

"Helping her was a good start."

"I'd help her with anything, but she doesn't need me. Not like she used to."

Audrey's eyes widened as something behind Austin caught her attention. He spun around, unsure of what he'd find, and his breath caught in his throat when he saw Harper standing there. She looked as beautiful as ever in the light of the moon.

"I still need you."

———

HOW LONG HAD Harper wanted Austin to look at her the way he was right now? It felt like an eternity. And now that he was, Harper was drawn into his amber eyes like a lifeline. She registered Audrey's departure back toward the inn, but barely.

"How much of that did you hear?" he asked.

Harper tucked her hair behind her ear. "I got here somewhere around Jennifer going off the deep end."

Austin took a step toward her, and her heart gave a little stutter. "So you know I never liked her? That it was always you?"

"I want to believe that, but…" She looked at the ground, her feet almost hidden in the thick grass.

Austin reached out and grabbed her hand. "Why was it so easy for you to believe that I was with Jennifer, but not that I'd spent the last four years wishing I'd done everything differently in college and ended up with you?"

"It's easy to believe because Jennifer is the type of girl you always fell for in college. It was easy to believe because you didn't even try to talk to me in the years since graduation." She felt her face heat up and was thankful for the poor lighting by the barn.

"I was an idiot for dating other girls when the perfect one was under my nose the entire time. I was even more of an idiot for letting this go on for so long. I love you."

Harper shook her head. "You can't say that. It's not fair when you're leaving in a few days to go back to LA. And before you bring up those baking lessons, I—"

"I quit."

She couldn't quite believe what she was hearing. "What?"

"I realized it was getting in the way of my dreams."

Harper's cheeks felt impossibly warmer, and her hands started to tremble at her sides. "But working in television *is* your dream."

He shook his head and took another step toward her. "You're my dream, Harper Hudson."

Impossible.

"What about your career? Where are you going to live?"

He shrugged. "I don't know yet."

"What? No plan?" She frowned.

A half-smile spread across his face. "If you can change, I can change."

"I haven't changed that much. Putting plates away properly and paying taxes on time isn't that hard. But you...Austin, you *always* need a plan."

He shook his head. "Not this time. I don't need a plan when I have you."

Harper's heart melted right then and there. She closed the distance between them with a few steps, leaned in and pressed her lips against Austin's. This time, there was no holding back, and she put her whole heart into it.

Austin was here, and they didn't have a plan, but she knew they could figure it out together. And they would because they'd spent too much time apart to let pesky details like where he would live or work get in the way. Of course she'd help him find a place to live. Of course he could help in her bakery until he figured things out. Planning this was easy.

She put the emotion she bottled up over the past four years into her kiss, and Austin's passion matched hers in every way.

Harper never wanted it to end, but eventually Austin pulled back and looked down at her longingly. "I love you so——"

Austin was interrupted by a fist colliding with his face.

Harper jumped back and screamed at the shadowy form moving in front of her to stand over Austin where he'd fallen on the ground. She couldn't see him well, but he was a big brute of a man, his hair a massive tangle of brown over wide, powerful shoulders.

She shoved her hand in her pocket, frantically trying to find her phone so she could call the police. But the monster spoke before she could find it.

"Get your paws off my sister."

Shock rippled through Harper's very core.

"Milo?"

Acknowledgments

Daphne and Kayla would like to thank their husbands for putting up with their crazy, and their kids for being so darn adorable.

Thank you Designed with Grace for this amazing cover.

Thank you EditElle for proofreading this book.

And to our AMAZING readers, thank you for letting us keep this dream alive.

About the Authors

Daphne and Kayla have been writing buddies since 2017.

They have three joint series together, but this is their first cowriting project.

Between the two of them they have: four kids, three cats, two husbands, and one fierce love of writing.

Kayla wishes she could eat tacos every day, and Daphne will never turn down free cake.

You can find them online at:

www.daphnejameshuff.com

www.tirrellblewrites.com